Wylde
Jan Irving

Dreamspinner Press

Published by
Dreamspinner Press
4760 Preston Road
Suite 244-149
Frisco, TX 75034
http://www.dreamspinnerpress.com/

Wylde

Cover Art by Paul Richmond   http://www.paulrichmondstudio.com

ISBN: 978-1-61581-374-2

Printed in the United States of America
First Edition
December, 2009

eBook edition available
eBook ISBN: 978-1-61581-375-9

Thanks to Carolyn, Laurie, Armandyouidiot,
Vikingprincess, Kim, Gabrielle, Missus Grace,
Lyn, Camjakefan, Habemus.
And Sedonia for meditation lessons.

In order to discover new lands, one must be willing to lose sight of the shore for a very long time.

—Anonymous

Chapter 1

JOSH MATTHEWS undid his safety belt and shoved open the passenger door of their Toyota Tundra truck, his eyes rounding as he took in the house surrounded by tall Western red cedars and Douglas firs, the moss-hung, impenetrable woods. "Dad!" he exclaimed, glancing at Noah with just a trace of the smile Noah treasured in the serious gray eyes he'd inherited from his father.

It was not an expression Noah had seen a lot of lately, so he took it as a good sign.

"Yeah," Noah said, smiling back. It would be okay. He was still shaky, but he was doing his best to hide it from Josh. And pretty soon he wouldn't just be acting the part of someone who was okay, he'd actually feel it. "Not bad, huh? Your old man found us, uh, a place with potential."

Josh, who was twelve now and growing so fast Noah got a pang in his gut at the thought of one day losing his little boy to the full-fledged teen years, walked up the cracked driveway to the gray rectangular box cradled between spurs of raw granite on Sullivan's Mountain.

Noah had purchased the house on a crazy impulse one day when he just needed to get out of Seattle. He hoped being surrounded by mists, bald eagles, olive-plumed trees and rare blue skies would do the trick. Built in the 1960s, the house was situated on the level part of a circular drive where the two nearest neighbors lived in dips in the road, naturally caused by free-running creeks.

He followed his son around the side of the house to the purple cement swimming pool with green rocks and a dicey hot tub. Despite the strange color, he thought maybe if it were landscaped in a less jarring shade and repaired, it might be a jewel. Anyway, he'd dreamed as soon as his realtor had faxed him photos of it. The tub could be used all winter even higher on the mountain, since the climate in Washington State usually ran more to rain than piles of snow.

Josh bent down and checked the water temperature, his forehead creased. "Nice. Dad, it's swim temperature! Even if the color.... Uh."

Noah shook his head. "I know. Can you bear it for a while? I had Jade Moreton warm it up for us since I thought even if it's ugly, we could use it," Noah said, referring to the local girl he'd hired to take care of the house. He was pleased Josh had noticed that the water was inviting, at least. He very much wanted his son to like their new life. And he'd worried about him for weeks, since moving a kid from established friends and schooling wasn't to be taken lightly. "There should even be a hot meal waiting inside—along with pie and coffee."

Like his Dad, Josh had a thing for berry pies, hot and fresh from the oven or microwaved so the juices sizzled. That and coffee made with dark, oily beans was pure heaven.

Josh grinned at his father. "Organic, right? Yeah, I could eat. Hey, can I back the truck closer to the house? We'll need to unload all those files you insisted on bringing...." His son rolled his eyes at how many home office supplies they'd carted on the drive down from Seattle, although Noah had pointed out that they had no idea when they'd be back at one of the big box stores.

Noah laughed, shaking his head. Josh's latest thing was working on his Dad to allow him to drive as often as possible. His kid couldn't wait to be sixteen—but Noah could. "Nuh uh. You're a few years short of doing any driving."

"But we're up in the wilderness, Dad! What if there was an emergency or something and you were injured and couldn't drive?" Josh followed Noah to the single peeling white door with a horseshoe hanging upside-down above it. So far Noah didn't think the house had been lucky, but he hoped to change that.

Josh bit his lip and hesitated before asking in a tiny voice, "And what if what happened to the family that used to live here happened to us?"

"What? Josh!" Noah rubbed the back of his neck. Okay, his son was smart and technically savvy; he must have Googled their new home and neighborhood. "Nothing happened to that family. I was told they needed to move closer to the city to make a living."

"I know the realtor told you that." Josh had a stubborn set to his chin. "But one of their kids posted on his blog that he was scared to live here…."

"Josh." Noah took a deep breath, his pride and excitement clouded. He didn't want to talk about their home's previous owners. He wanted to show off their brand new perfect life to his son. This was where Noah intended to regain his independence, where he intended to make his stand.

Josh studied his father, gray eyes grave. "Sorry, Dad. I'm really happy to be here. Can I open the door with the new key?"

Noah handed him the shiny gold key, which was in better repair than their front door. "Keep it; that one's yours. And as for the driving… we'll discuss it sometime." Noah threw Josh a bone to thank him for dropping the topic. Much as he hated to admit it, his son had a point about driving anyway. This wasn't the busy 'burbs of Seattle. Josh might need a few survival skills in this more remote part of the country. "Just promise me one thing, 'kay?"

"Yeah, what's that?" Josh breezed through the foyer and made a beeline for the oak- and brass-appointed kitchen with its stone hearth and hanging copper pots. Noah had already had someone working in the kitchen, even before they moved in. It would be the first room they'd renovate.

"Don't go into the woods without me and a really good map," Noah commanded. He glanced out the long kitchen windows and swallowed, since the one thing that made him uneasy sometimes about his new home was that thick forest. It was stupid, but he guessed it was because he was an urban man. "You could get lost out there."

Josh looked out at the tall cedar and fir trees that towered over their new home. "No worries. It looks cold and wet and I'd hate to be lost out there."

Noah sighed. Would Josh like where they had moved or not?

HE WAS hungry. And cold. And shivering.

From the bluff above the small gray box, he watched the boy and man walk around the house. Watched the man put his hand on the boy's shoulder at one point, squeezing with what looked like affection.

He made a soft sound, remembering his grandpa. He'd cared about him. Long... long time ago. And thinking about him made his head hurt and his heart race and tears sting his eyes.

He could smell the hot food inside that house.

IT WAS late, and Jade Moreton knew she had to get home soon. She had night school the next evening right after a double shift at the diner, which felt kind of shitty since sometimes it seemed like all she did was work.

And what she wanted was to get laid.

Trouble was, she'd had all the eligible men in town. Well, all but two.

Right now she was bent over the john, scrubbing Thomas Anderson's en suite. The inquisitive rich teen was lucky enough to live in this posh house, renovated out of the shell of an old bungalow, up on Sullivan's Mountain. He was leaning against the doorway, watching her work, probably staring at her ass, but he was all right. She was firm with him that she didn't play around with kids, but since he'd been to all kinds of fancy places like Paris and Rome, he was fun to talk to.

Jade had always wanted to travel, leave this mudball boring town behind. She loved looking at Thomas's computer photo albums of places he'd visited, listening to his stories of Bangladesh or Sydney, Australia. She knew someone else who had traveled, though it had been in the army, not as a pampered kid. Actually, nothing about Deputy Alec Danvers looked pampered, and she would know, since they shared the same gym—the *only* gym in small-town Sullivan.

And why was she thinking about him again? Despite how he had come back and was almost a celebrity at their foothills village, he was nothing to Jade, just another man. She'd lived in this hick town with a higher boys-to-girls ratio all her life, so she'd learned a thing or two, and one of them was she didn't want to end up like her foster mother, a single parent working in a crap-ass diner all her life.

She studied hard, and she played hard, but on *her* terms.

She'd lost her virginity at sixteen and never regretted it, but she'd been careful even then to make sure the boy wore a condom. She was not getting knocked up and knocked down. No, sir!

"You heading up for a swim?" Thomas asked, smiling hopefully. "You don't need to use that old pool at the empty house. Ours is pretty cool. And new."

Jade shook her head, figuring that seventeen-year-old Thomas wanted to see her in her suit. Well, forget that.

She watched him take another hit of the very fine grass he no doubt got from Morley Orris, the local pot farmer. No way could she afford that shit, and she didn't take it when he offered, since she was fairly sure she might lose her job if she got too cozy with the favored son. She was the twice-a-week maid, pure and simple, and Thomas's mom was not a lady you'd want to tangle with. His father was even worse, cold with Jade, spending his free time when he was home fishing or hunting. "I wish I could, Thomas. Nice of you to ask," Jade said with some regret. She didn't have long before she had to head back and cover her friend Marcie Hollis for an hour down at the diner. Just enough time to visit the pool belonging to the new Seattle folks, which was a quick walk through the woods.

She unfolded her six-foot frame from the bathroom floor, finished for the day, catching her reflection in Thomas's newly polished mirror. She liked what she saw, sun-streaked brown hair and toned body.

"That place gives me the creeps," Thomas observed.

"Why do you say that?" Jade poured her pail of dirty water into his toilet and then flushed it while Thomas took another lazy hit.

"It was weird, the family just disappearing one night, as if they were scared off or something, though I guess since Ralph Hindle got hurt and died in the woods, they probably didn't like it here much anymore. He was a cool guy, used to come around here all the time…." Thomas shrugged. "Before they lived there, the place was empty since the old man who built it keeled over from a heart attack. So yeah, the house seems like bad luck."

Jade shrugged, already anticipating a cool dip to get rid of the miasma of cleaning for other people and to ease her sore back muscles. "Well, pool. And I remember the first owner. He wasn't creepy, just old." She was amused. "He was really into gardening, that's for sure, even had his grandson help him out sometimes, though the place has grown all wild now."

"I better walk with you as far as the house," Thomas offered, butting out his grass. "Don't want the ghost of Sullivan's Mountain to get you."

Jade held his gaze, making sure he knew there would be nothing more than walking involved. "Okay." She didn't want to hurt his manly pride by pointing out she could take care of herself.

BUT when they broke through the meadow, which was full of buttercups, foxglove, and wild daisies this time of year, Jade and Thomas spotted some lights on and a big Toyota truck taking possession of the uneven old driveway.

"Should you ring their bell or something?" Thomas asked, hesitating.

Jade shook her head, having only spoken to Noah Matthews on the phone. He had said she could use the pool whenever she wanted, but she didn't want to interrupt his first day in a new home.

"There's a road through the woods they used when they were cutting out the lots," Thomas suggested, as if reading her disappointment. "It's not paved and it's a bit rough, overgrown, but it'll take us around the house. We can hike through the trees 'til we get to the pool."

Jade wanted to give him a queenly pat on the cheek, happy to be catered to. It was something she intended to get used to, something she intended to live for real one day. A vision of Alec Danvers, tall and tanned with floppy brown hair, rose in her mind's eye. He seemed perfectly content in this small corner. But something like this would never be enough for Jade. She'd make her way somehow.

NOAH watched Josh looking around his room. The movers had brought everything a couple of weeks back, and Noah had driven out to the country to supervise the unpacking. He'd spent particular time in this room, hoping it would mean the closeness he'd once

7

enjoyed with his son would return. Of course, he knew why they weren't close, and it wasn't *Josh* who had pulled away. It was Noah.

He sighed, rubbing the back of his neck.

As Noah watched, Josh passed a reverent hand over the handsome walnut desk and Dell laptop he'd treated him with. Noah hoped it made up for the chilly, cracked granite-tiled floor and dark, unknown scrap wood that made up the walls. Josh's bedroom was on the bottom level, near the kitchen, but it was cold and, when Noah had first seen it, full of cobwebs and wolf spiders. The ugly things freaked him out a little. "Not bad," Josh noted, amusement in his eyes. "Dad, a new computer and not a stupid desktop!"

"Not bad? Hell of a lot better than I had growing up!" Noah pointed out, shaking his head. But he'd never wanted hard times for his kid. He was grateful that the money his wife had left them, supplemented by his work writing technical manuals for software engineers, meant he'd been able to provide better.

"Yeah, yeah. Poor boy makes good." Josh rolled his eyes. Then he bit his lip. His face looked very young to Noah as he continued, "I wish... Mom could see it. Do you think she can, maybe?"

Josh was very grown-up for his age, but the topic of his mother could sometimes leave him grasping for extra reassurance.

Noah didn't believe in traditional religion, so he sat down, giving himself a moment. He always wanted to say the right thing, the weight of being a single parent heavy. "I think that wherever she is, she'd like to know we're happy, that's what I think, Joshua."

Josh nodded, satisfied for the moment. "But who are you going to date out here, Dad? I mean, you're still pretty young."

Noah felt a blush coming on at his son's frankness. That was one topic he wanted to stay away from! Until recently, he'd lived like a monk since Margaret's death from cancer all those years ago. Raising his son and working like a demon to lose himself in his job and bury his loneliness had taken all his time—well, until a few months ago.

Uneasiness tightened his shoulders. *Don't think about it.*

He cleared his throat, embarrassed that his heartbeat accelerated. He paused before continuing, again aching to be truthful with his son about so many things… but was Josh ready to know who his father truly was? Noah was too shaky to confide in him— yet. But he hoped some time out here in their new life would change that. "Maybe I'll meet someone right at the church social," he teased with forced lightness.

"Ha ha, yeah, right. Do they still do those things out in the country?" Josh asked, eyes wide, as if he were an anthropologist studying a strange culture.

That look made Noah smile. Shit, he was glad that when Margaret got pregnant from a one-nighter, they'd decided to have Josh, to be married. She'd never been what he'd wanted, but they'd created this amazing person.

Noah shook his head full of carefully styled ash-blond hair. "I don't know. All I know about the country I learned from watching *Dr. Quinn, Medicine Woman* with you when you were younger."

THOMAS shone his small flashlight into the deep woods off the tiny, rugged road. "I think if we head through there it shouldn't be too far."

"Okay," Jade agreed. "But you can go back if you want; your Mom might want you."

Thomas's face tightened. He and his mother didn't get on well, Jade guessed. Well, the woman was a real dragon with an icy temper, although not as chilly as her husband. "Doubt it. You know this is a total cliché, don't you?"

"It is?" Jade paused to study Thomas, thinking he wasn't such a bad kid, just bored and unhappy. She could certainly remember feeling that way herself.

"I mean, two hot young people heading into the scary abandoned old house or the haunted woods...." Thomas lifted some dry hanging moss in one hand, which was suspended from a dead, bleached branch, reaching out like a skeletal hand. "Every horror movie I ever saw, the kids who have sex wind up dead."

"Okay, one, Thomas," Jade scoffed. "There will be no sex. Second, that's probably a cliché based on prudish Judeo-Christian ideas that being hot was a bad thing."

Thomas blinked as if impressed.

"All the night school I'm taking," Jade confessed, flushing a little. He could totally choose whatever school he attended, but Jade, not so much. "But to tell you the truth, kid, this mountain always gave me the creeps. If I had a shit load of dough, I wouldn't live up here, nuh uh."

Still, she led the way into the damp breath of the trees, watching her footing carefully, since she'd grown up on hiking trails on the Pacific Northwest. Roots and rocks could snag an unwary walker, and she had a scar on one knee from a fall on unforgiving granite.

The only beacon came from Thomas's heavy flashlight, piercing the olive gloom and guiding them over a rough trail, like something animals used through the brush. Mist writhed over the trees and shrubs, which were damp and dripping with the late spring night air.

"Hey... did you see that?" Thomas asked her suddenly, startling her.

Ice feathered down her back again. Jade frowned, ignoring it. "See what? I think we must be almost at the pool."

Thomas's voice was bemused. "I just thought I saw someone moving up ahead there."

Jade swallowed, suddenly dry-mouthed. This was stupid; she was acting like a kid who had played with an Ouija board at a sleepover. Besides, she was the adult, so she had to reassure Thomas. But suddenly this simple walk to take a dip seemed like a bad idea. "Do black bears wander around at night up here?" she asked. Where she lived in the foothills, although it was remote and countrified, it was unusual to see one.

"Sometimes they get into our garbage. In fact, the other night one really fucked up our cans. Dad bought some heavy-duty bearproof metal ones, but something got into it anyway!" Thomas shared. "Probably the fucking ghost that lives up here."

"Crap!" Jade gave a relieved laugh.

"What?"

"You're trying to scare me. Come on, admit it."

"Actually...." Thomas paused and then shone the light up toward his face, his pale skin, green eyes, and mousy brown hair looking extra washed out in the diffuse misty air. "I seriously wouldn't mind heading back. I, uh, think we might be lost."

"But the house is just ahead. We could make out the lights through the woods just a minute ago!" Jade put her hands on her hips, a little scared for her charge. She hadn't meant for him to join her, get lost up here with her. And if she didn't return to her car soon, she'd miss helping Marcie out with that extra hour her girlfriend needed this evening with her kids. Shit!

"Yeah, but the trail kind of snaked deeper into the woods. I think we somehow missed the house and pool," Thomas said, uneasiness in his voice.

Well, hell, she was uneasy too, though she hated to admit there was anything she wasn't up to handling. She took a deep breath. "Okay, I guess we should walk back, retrace our steps. It's not far, is it? I never wandered around here all the time I've worked in the house."

11

"I don't think so," Thomas said, sounding eager to follow her plan.

"All right, let's do it then, come on. I'm going to be in so much shit tonight if I'm really late. My girlfriend needed some extra time to see her son's exhibit at the library art show."

Jade skidded down a leaf-covered hill, careful not to slide on the mud and wind up on her ass. Behind her, Thomas's flashlight lit their path, weaving back and forth like the flashlights used on a paranormal investigation TV show.

She turned to check on Thomas's progress when suddenly, the flashlight flickered. Went out!

"Oh, *fuck!*" he muttered. "I knew I shoulda got new batteries."

Jade wrapped her arms around herself, worried because without light, they had no way to find their way back. "Okay, maybe we should...." She swallowed, *not* wanting to suggest this plan, but maybe it truly was their only option. "Just stay here. Huddle somewhere together and wait until it gets light out. We should be able to find our way then." She made herself sound confident so he wouldn't be scared.

"I don't know; we weren't too far from the road...." Thomas's voice drifted off, and Jade could tell he was no more wild than she was about spending the rest of the night out here in the forest, waiting for the light to break.

Jade chewed her lip, tempted. All they needed was to make out the house lights again, and they were home free....

She reached out and felt for Thomas's sleeve. "Hang on to me, okay? Your Mom will be really pissed if I don't get you home in one piece."

"Don't worry, Jade; I brought more than a flashlight," Thomas confessed, voice grim. "I got my Dad's gun handy."

"*What?*" Jade barked.

IN HIS study, Noah put on his glasses and went over some the hard copy he'd printed out of his next book. He found it easier to catch little mistakes if he read the work in his favorite chair. It was late, but the excitement of finally being here after months of planning kept him wide awake.

But had they moved for the best reason? The thought had raised itself more than once like a persistent ghost, but now, not wanting to think about what had led to his decision, Noah got up and opened the peeling French doors, letting in the cool mountain air. The lights were on around the pool—the ones that were still working and not broken or buried by debris—highlighting the unkempt landscaping, but beyond was the sheer dark volume of the woods, seeming to loom oppressively over tall green grass and sculpted rock.

He frowned, remembering Josh's unease with the surrounding forest. He wondered if his son would come to like where they lived, their new environment—so far he'd been very fixated on the new props of their life, but Noah had made a deliberate effort to sweeten the pot until they could fix up their home. To Noah, their new surroundings were soothing, even though sometimes he saw them in a different light, as if looking at the skull of a person through their skin. But he knew he and Josh just weren't used to this much natural land. It was nothing like where they'd come from.

As he listened to the waterfall spilling down into the broken purple pool, he felt his shoulders relaxing.

AT THE diner, Chief Kell Farraday touched his radio and called back County Deputy Alec Danvers, who sometimes offered him welcome backup here in Sullivan, which had a small population of just over one thousand two hundred.

The deputy was currently dealing with a drunk and disorderly, Moss Beacon over at the Road House again. His old lady cheated on him, and instead of giving her hell, Moss picked a fight with someone every Friday night regular, taking out his frustration on travelers since the locals were too smart to mix it up with him.

"Does he need stitches this time, Alec?" Kell asked his friend, grateful for his help. He'd started the day with administration work he had to cover since his secretary was only part-time, delved into a felony investigation, and then topped his time off with doing traffic duty for a bike-a-thon through town.

"Naw, but the guy he hit sure does! Looks like he was mowed down by a truck, Chief."

Kell sighed. Well, that made things more complicated. Why the hell couldn't Moss think things through? "The guy he fought want to press charges?"

"He's out cold, Chief. Want me to ask him when he comes to?"

"Yeah, you do that," Kell drawled. "Meanwhile I'm going to have a nice big piece of peach pie." This was his favorite part of the unpredictable day of a local chief. He made less money than a starting patrolman in most parts of the country, but he liked this town. And this town liked him: They were satisfied, along with the board, with his work, and willing to overlook his personal life. And living here, he knew just about everyone. It also gave a man lots of thinking time, which Kell liked. He was a natural loner, and a couple things in town the past couple of years had made him thoughtful. But he just knew one day he'd get to the bottom of it, like the so-called ghost haunting Sullivan's forest.

"Kell...." Marcie Hollis, a single mother who worked the diner, was at his elbow, her brow wrinkled, her red hair in a band off her face.

"Yes, ma'am?" Kell asked, ever calm and polite, but something in Marcie's expression made him light up, instinctively

14

thinking maybe he wouldn't be having pie and coffee in peace tonight.

"Jade was going to cover my shift for the last hour." Marcie shifted her feet, which were probably sore and swollen. Here was someone else who made her living the hard way.

Kell gave Marcie a comprehensive look, letting her know that he was aware Jade Moreton stayed out late some nights.

"No, Kell, she's completely reliable about work and she never breaks a promise to a friend," Marcie said, clearly worried.

"She up working on Sullivan's Mountain?" The houses were still technically close enough to be part of the town, so it was under his jurisdiction, though right now only two families lived up there.

"Yes sir, at the Anderson place today, I think." Marcie went over to the strawberry pie under the dome and stuck one in a plastic package, handing it to Kell as thanks as he got up, abandoning his half-finished coffee.

"Well, I'll drive on up and see if I can find her, okay?"

"THANK you," Marcie said, genuinely grateful; he was such a good man. She wished Kell weren't gay. Not that everyone knew, since he was discreet, probably going to another town to do his prowling, but she was the former town bad girl. If Kell had liked pussy, she figured she would have known by now.

Damn, what a waste, she thought as she watched his nicer-than-average ass as he walked out the door.

SOMETHING cold and soft brushed Jade's arm. She gasped, startled, before realizing it was a damn branch! "Thomas, you okay?" Oh, shit, they were totally lost, and she knew Thomas was spooked, which, adding in the gun, was not a good thing. He was convinced someone was up here with them in the woods.

Thomas's hand jerked from Jade's grip.

It was so dark she couldn't make anything out, but she thought she heard something breathing.

"Thomas, where are you?"

NOAH snapped out the light in his office, rubbing his eyes tiredly. He had better get some rest. He was looking forward to breakfast out on the cracked cement of the patio if it were warm enough in the morning. Maybe he and Noah could talk like they used to, before—

Bam!

The sound sent a cold chill down Noah's back. He snapped on the light again and went to the open doors, peering into the night.

Josh clattered down the stairs from his bedroom, wearing PJs with the solar system on them, his eyes wide and terrified. "Dad! Someone's shooting in the woods!"

Chapter 2

"STAY here!" Noah ordered his son, who was standing close beside him. "I want to take a look out there." But his heart was pounding; he really didn't. Still, he couldn't have Josh afraid of their new home their first day under its roof! Had it really been a gunshot, or had he imagined it? Hell, he couldn't be sure it wasn't a kid with a firecracker!

"*No,* Dad! Please, don't go out there!"

Noah pushed Josh into his desk chair and cupped his shoulder, holding wide gray eyes. He had to suppress the urge to brush the ash-colored hair off Josh's forehead. "It's all lit up around the pool and probably this is just some kind of prank."

His son gave him a disbelieving look, but Noah squeezed his shoulder and then walked out the French doors. He had to show his son there was nothing to worry about, but he was a bit abashed that his heart continued to thud in his ears. He knew it was nothing, just some kids playing or something. They'd only just moved here, and they had yet to make the adjustment.

Once outside, he walked around the perimeter of the pool, lit to accent what remained of the landscaping. The woods surrounded the little oasis of the house and grounds, towering and hushed, cooling the air. Noah walked to the very edge of his property and peered into the shadows.

After a moment, not really seeing anything, he looked back over his shoulder to glimpse his son's face peering anxiously from the study window, watching his father. Doubts struck him again.

Why had he brought Josh out here? This bad first night seemed to grind his good intentions of a fresh start into dust.

He sighed, deciding to do one more circuit.

Something grabbed his arm—

CHIEF KELL FARRADAY shifted the gears in his marked official SUV as he began the curving drive up the slope that switch-backed through Sullivan's Mountain. He passed one house with glass windows that reflected the lights of his vehicle as he climbed higher.

He felt tension move through his shoulders as he drove, as if some primal warning system was standing at attention. Like most of the locals, he didn't like this mountain. He couldn't have said why, since one mountain was more or less the same as another around here, but there was something about *this* one, although he discounted the stories of a Sasquatch in the area, of course. But someone had lifted supplies from a fishing shack belonging to a friend of his, and someone had taken Mrs. Harrison's groceries right out of her driveway when she was carrying the bags two by two up to her kitchen.

The big truck slid to a screeching halt as he glimpsed light from a turnoff into the woods not far from the Anderson house where Jade Moreton had been scheduled to work today.

KELL shone his powerful flashlight at the back of the Lexus that was perched incongruously in the middle of the unpaved road. The forest loomed on either side of the trophy car, crowding and oddly watchful.

The headlights were still on. Kell checked the door and found it unlocked, the keys still in the ignition.

Gravel crunching under a footfall.

He swung around, his Ranger's instincts in full battle mode—

His flashlight spotlighted Marisa Anderson, Thomas's mother. She was leaving the woods with Albert Newton, who owned the general store in town. Oh ho. She flushed on seeing the Chief, but went on the offensive right off. "Is there some problem, Kell?" she demanded, raising a pale blonde brow.

"No problem, I'm just looking for Jade Moreton," Kell said, not particularly interested in what Marisa was doing with Albert in the woods. In his town, there were a lot of secrets. A lot of people spending time in beds not their own. Much simpler to be gay, he thought. Go, hit some tight ass in another bigger town, and be done with it. "I called your house but only got the answering machine."

"I'm sure I have no idea where Jade is. She merely cleans my house," Marisa dismissed. She held Kell's gaze with cold eyes. She wasn't a woman he'd like to cross, frankly, since he had the feeling she'd find a way to settle with him, and he didn't need the aggravation. He'd heard she was the second wife of the very wealthy Mr. Anderson and she intended to stay that way, despite the rumors that she fooled around on the side.

Of course, Mr. Anderson wasn't a man to mess with either. He was an experienced hunter and fisherman who had a short temper. He had once threatened one of the men in town for drunkenly admiring his wife at a party.

Now Kell watched Marisa Anderson climb into her car, perfectly calm though her pink silk shirt was on inside out. Albert avoided Kell's searching gaze; he was also married, with four children. He slid into the passenger side.

"Mrs. Anderson." Kell called her by her last name, irritated, but hiding it. "Did Jade happen to mention where she might be going? She never showed at work and it's unlike her."

She slammed her door closed, obviously reading his poorly disguised disapproval. "I believe she used to visit the pool at the abandoned house sometimes."

Albert sang out, "It's not abandoned! Someone bought it a couple of months ago." He looked at Kell. "And we heard something just a while back, Kell. Some kind of noise, like a firecracker. Scared the shit out of me, I can tell you!"

"Noise...." A firecracker could sound like gunfire also. Kell hoped to hell a firecracker was all it was.

Marisa gave Kell a cold look, no doubt partially because she'd importuned him more than once and he'd ignored her. "Could you move your vehicle please?"

AS HE watched Marisa's headlights wink out behind a switchback, Kell paused, looking up the road. If Jade had come up here to use the pool, she might have hiked this road.

Kell cupped a hand to his mouth. *"Jade? This is Chief Farraday!"*

There was no response, but Kell heard the crackle of brush just ahead and saw something slink across the road: a coyote with upright ears and a deep chest, good-sized. Its eyes shone yellow and demonic in the beam of Kell's flashlight before it disappeared with a snarl.

"Huh. Nice puppy," Kell muttered to himself. Well, he was coming up dry on finding Jade. Then, he noticed that the coyote had headed up the old construction road used when the houses on this part of the bluff were built. It was full of saplings and brush, but it led deep into the woods.

Could Jade have somehow gone that way?

DEPUTY ALEC DANVERS drove up the first curve at the base of the mountain on his regular patrol route, which overlapped the town of Sullivan. The bundle in deerskin his part-Haida grandmother had given him felt oddly warm against the skin of his neck. She'd insisted he carry it when he wound up with this patrol, though she hadn't said exactly why that was, other than he'd need strength.

Alec didn't believe in the old ways, but for some reason he'd gotten in the habit of carrying it, especially after the Hindles had abruptly moved away, reportedly because they were scared of the ghost that was reputed to haunt these woods.

When he'd been in town, about to take his break at the diner and spend some time looking mildly in Jade Moreton's direction, he'd heard Kell had gone up there looking for her.

So of course he'd gotten in his truck and followed.

RELUCTANTLY, Kell went into the woods, still calling periodically for Jade. Something felt off. Why hadn't she responded? He was worried she'd had some kind of accident up here, perhaps involving the possible gunfire. Had a hunter taken a shot at her?

He stepped over some rocks and his hand reached out to steady his passage, grasping a young tree. Something about the texture caught his attention, and he directed his flashlight on it: something wet. Something fresh.

Instinctively, using instincts honed to hunt men, Kell brought his damp finger to his lips, tasting—

Blood.

He backed away to take a closer look and stumbled over something soft and still, lying crumpled on the ground.

"SHIT!" Noah barked as he took a swing at whatever had him by the arm.

"*Easy,* tiger! You really don't want to hit the local lawman," a silky voice warned him.

Noah dropped his arm and stared at the tall stranger. "I… what are you doing out here?"

"I was searching for a missing waitress, and I found her just now. I'm Chief Kell Farraday."

The man loomed over Noah, his face burned brown and weathered by the elements. He was wearing a serviceable uniform with a shoulder patch bearing the embroidery *Town of Sullivan Police.* His chocolate hair had streaks of white at the temples, but despite that, it feathered boyishly over his forehead. His eyes were so dark that Noah couldn't make out the pupils. *Predator's eyes.* He shivered a little at the bizarre thought.

"A missing woman? My God, we heard something like gunfire from the woods. I was just out here seeing if I could find the source." Noah followed the other man into the forest, feeling oddly comforted by the presence of this stranger with big hands and a confident air. It made the past few minutes seem… almost fanciful. It hadn't been anything strange going on, just someone who had been hurt.

The Chief stopped and put his hands on his lean hips, and Noah saw why he'd looked for help. A young woman lay unconscious on the forest floor. The ground around her was torn up.

"Oh, my!" Noah cried out, immediately concerned.

"Yep. Can you run back to your house and call an ambulance? My radio and phone seem to be out because the reception up here's not working for some reason and I'm reluctant to move her until I know how she was injured," the Chief outlined. "She could have hurt her neck or back and require special attention." The lawman knelt to touch the woman's cool cheek gently. "She seems to be bruised and unconscious, possibly from that bump on her forehead."

NOAH sprinted back to the house. The contrast between the dark, chilly woods and even his primitively landscaped yard was as stark as the North Pole to Hawaii.

"Dad?" Josh hovered as he made the call, reaching out to touch Noah's arm, as if needing that physical reassurance.

"It's okay, Josh. I found out who was in the woods—a young woman suffered some kind of accident, but I don't believe she was shot." Noah put an arm around Josh, and his son allowed it. "She was breathing, just unconscious. I'm hoping she'll be fine."

Josh looked out the window at the forest. "I'm glad. Uh, you weren't in the kitchen before you came to talk to me, were you?"

Noah blinked at the strange question. "No. Why do you ask?"

"The pie and food we had waiting for supper… it's gone, Dad. Looks like someone walked in the kitchen and took it."

A DEPUTY showed up at Noah's front door first, Alec Danvers. He barely spoke to Noah before heading off into the woods at a run. Then, twenty minutes later, the ambulance arrived. The young woman turned out to be Jade Moreton, who had cleaned up the house for Noah and Josh. Noah had spoken to her several times on the phone and found her efficient and pleasant. She was carefully retrieved and put on a stretcher.

"KELL, Thomas left me a note on the fridge that he was going to escort that girl Jade to your pool," Marisa Anderson, Noah's new neighbor, told the big lawman as soon as Noah let her into his great room. "I've called around and he's not with any of his friends. I'm afraid he might still be up there, in the woods…." Her jaw tightened, but otherwise her face remained expressionless. "Perhaps he got lost, trying to find help for her."

Kell nodded as he listened, looking grim. "It's very easy to get turned around up there in the dark. I'll call and see if I can get added back up from two more of the county deputies. We'll search around the house."

Marisa's face thawed slightly as she gave a perfunctory nod.

NOAH played host to Marisa Anderson, who for some reason looked uncomfortable under his roof. Was it because this rundown old house was nothing like the showplace she'd renovated? Or was it because of what he'd caught one of the deputies whispering about her, that she'd had an affair with a man who used to live here? Whatever it was, it blurred by Noah since he was still adjusting to his first night here.

Kell caught his eye, and Noah followed him to the peeling French doors.

"I could really use another pair of eyes," the Chief said. "Any warm body."

"I might get as lost as that boy," Noah admitted ruefully. "But I'll go with you, of course."

As he stepped out onto the patio, he glanced back toward his cozy kitchen, at Marisa Anderson sitting at his battered farmhouse table, hands clenched around the hot cup of coffee Josh had made her.

"THANKS for coming along," the Chief told Noah, adding, "Some house you bought, a real fixer-upper." They were combing the land above where Noah's home was located. The ground was covered with snake-like roots, loose rock, and protruding shards of granite. Both men moved carefully in the darkness, though the Chief seemed to have a special grace, treading almost soundlessly.

24

Noah blinked at the other man, finding it surreal that on his first day in his new home, he was out in the woods, searching for a lost boy. "I thought country life might agree with my son. You know, peace and quiet, Chief?" His lips quirked grimly, and the other man gave him a steady glance, as if he were still weighing Noah.

"Yep, it's usually like that. By the way, call me Kell," the Chief suggested absently. He touched Noah's lower back to guide him over some deadfall on the deer trail they were following before ranging ahead, listening, testing the ground for uneven footing. The forest crowded them on either side, but Noah didn't experience the fear he'd felt earlier, and he knew it was because of this man. The lawman had a quiet air of capability.

"Were you in the army?" he asked on a hunch.

Kell gave him a surprised glance. "Yeah, Army Rangers. Guess it still shows some, huh?"

"Yes," Noah said. "I hope it won't make me seem unmacho, but I admit I wouldn't want to walk these woods alone at night."

Kell shook his head, grim. "Me neither."

"Chief...." Noah flushed under the steady gaze. "Kell. Something odd happened, other than the strange sound that I hope very much was a firecracker."

"Um?" Kell prodded, gaze on the trail.

"Someone, uh, stole our dinner."

"Lot of that going around, on and off, over the years. Some folks think it's a ghost."

"What do you think?"

Kell shook his head. "I have no idea, but I didn't think ghosts ate food."

"YOU seem familiar with this path."

"Walked it before when someone else was missing hereabouts."

Wide-eyed, Noah asked, "Someone *else* went missing?"

"Not anymore." Kell huffed up a granite bluff and looked around with narrowed eyes. Noah followed and saw a perfect view of his house, lit like a beacon in the heart of the dark woods. "Found his remains last fall. Name of Ralph Hindle, a relative of the folks who lived in your house before they lit out. Kind of a hippy type from the university, studying wildlife out here."

"He died in these woods?"

"Nope," Kell said laconically, turning back to delve back onto the trail. "Over on Morley Orris's property about a mile from here."

"Is he the man that Marisa Anderson had an affair with?" Noah probed.

"Huh. Didn't take long for you to pick up on that rumor. I have no idea. Her husband seems the possessive type so I might have looked at him, but Ralph seemed to have just gotten lost, hurt... and then died before we could find him."

Noah swallowed dryly, abruptly sickened. "I... didn't know anyone had died nearby."

"Realtor didn't tell you, huh? Well, he had a house to sell and yours has a bit of an unfortunate history, starting with old Mr. Butler, the man who built it, dying of a heart attack. Folks didn't find him for a while...."

"Well, maybe the Hindles didn't want to stay after their relative died out here. And it is in questionable repair. I'm probably going to have to replace everything," Noah said morosely.

"Uh huh." The Chief was noncommittal.

"How did this man Hindle die?"

"Coroner said it was an animal attack, but there wasn't enough of him left to tell."

Noah was suddenly angry. He snagged Kell's arm. "Are you telling me this to frighten the city slicker, Chief?"

Kell shook his head, apparently unruffled at Noah's show of spirit. He stared calmly at Noah's fingers until Noah removed them. "You've got quite the temper, but I think I like that," Kell said in a thoughtful voice. "As for why I told you about Hindle, I just think you should be careful. This isn't exactly Walton's Mountain."

AN HOUR later, Kell addressed the exhausted searchers back on Noah's property. "Dawn is two hours away so I want you all to go home, get some rest, feed up and then come back tomorrow. We'll expand the perimeter then, have a better chance of finding Thomas in daylight."

THE young man watched the searchers leave from his hiding place under a dead tree. He didn't know if they were looking for him, but he was scared, and his stomach was cramped from eating a whole pie, filched from the new people. He put his head on his knees, shivering, wishing that, like that boy in the nearby house, he had someone who cared about him.

But there was no one he could let near him. No one he could trust.

NOAH watched the Chief staring at the trees beyond his large bay living room windows. "Shouldn't you sleep too?" he asked softly.

"Yeah. I have a blanket in the truck—"

"Absolutely not. I have a guest room, complete with razor. You're welcome to stay." Noah's eyes dropped to the other man's belt.

"Like something you see?" Kell's drawl was rough and tired.

"Excuse me?" Noah flushed.

"You keep staring at my crotch."

"I do not! It's your belt buckle; it's very distinctive." It was heavy silver, elaborately wrought, with undulating figures. It kept catching Noah's gaze, making him puzzle at the pattern.

"Uh huh." Kell scrubbed his eyes. "You gay?"

"I… I have a son," Noah said faintly, crossing his arms.

"So?" Kell prodded as he followed Noah to the offered room. "That just means you have viable sperm, not where you like to spill it."

Chapter 3

"ARE you hitting on me, Chief?" Noah demanded, crossing his arms.

"Surely men have hit on you before, you being from the big, bad city," Kell noted tiredly, not denying it.

"I can't believe how brash you are!" Noah told himself he was offended as the Chief looked at him with weary but appreciative eyes. But... hadn't he come out here so he could eventually be the man he'd always wanted to be? Of course, that didn't necessarily mean taking up with some macho local.

"You don't waste time out here in the country. Only so many bodies to tangle with in front of a fire and, as for attractive gay men...." Kell shrugged. "Not many. Besides, I'm picky."

"I have no idea why you'd think that I would be receptive to your advances," Noah shot, unable to think of how to handle confident Kell. His words were like hands stroking over Noah's skin. Noah told himself he was irritated, not.... He wasn't ready after his mistake in Seattle.

"Bullshit, you don't know!" Kell growled, leaning against the doorway of the borrowed room. "Listen, if I wasn't sure you were 'receptive', I sure as hell wouldn't tell you how I wish I could push you on your stomach on the guest bed and nail you while you scratch the sheets and beg for more."

Noah shook his head. "You're either a lunatic or a complete barbarian!"

29

Kell chuckled as Noah's gaze dropped to his crotch and then flew away when he realized he was doing it again. Despite how weary the Chief was, their disagreement had made him hard, pushing lustily against his zipper.

And that hardness kept attracting Noah's eye.

KELL knew he was way over the line of decent behavior, but something about Noah made him edgy, pissy, and horny as fuck. Normally he wasn't into city guys. He just wanted to get down and sweaty. No pretence. Sometimes he liked to tie his date up with his belt, if the man agreed, bend him over a couch or his SUV, and help himself.

The thought of doing that to Noah almost made him groan. Shit! He'd just met him, but apparently the uptight man rang his bell. *Hard.* Just his luck, since despite the vibes, Noah seemed in hiding for some reason, unlike Kell, who had had a belly full of that and now just wanted to be himself.

"I better lock up." Noah made to turn away, and Kell stopped him with a gentle hand cupping his elbow.

Noah caught his breath at the simple touch. *Oh, right, you're not gay.* Kell wanted to roll his eyes. "Sorry if I came on too strong," Kell surprised himself by saying. "I'm worried about that kid out there lost in the forest, but... I shouldn't have said all that shit."

Noah gave him a straight look under ash-blond brows. "But you meant it, didn't you?"

"Yeah."

"Then don't be sorry," Noah surprised the bigger man by saying.

Kell blinked, staring after Noah as he walked away. "Well... day-yam. Did he just *flirt* with me?" he muttered to himself.

AS SOON as he returned to his home office, a little shaken from his stirring encounter with the Chief—he was *not* going to dwell on it, but he'd liked that he'd managed to surprise the confident man—Noah noticed the French doors were still standing open, bringing in the night air like chilly incense. As he closed them, he thought about Josh's story that their food had gone missing. Strange. Had the kid lost in the woods somehow gotten in and snagged it as another part of a prank?

Noah looked out at the dark, towering stands of trees that he'd thought so pristine before moving here. Now there seemed to be an air of waiting menace, as if something watched the house from the shadows.

He shook off the strange fancy, blaming his son for making him think that. All right, it had been a bad start, but somehow they'd take it day by day and make this their home. God knew the house itself had plenty of room for improvement.

THE woods enveloped the young man like a familiar dark womb after he polished off the last of the stolen food, uncertain when he'd eat so well again. He'd been frightened when the gun had gone off—someone shooting at him? He didn't know, but this was his place.

He decided to investigate.

KELL checked his flashlight. He put a hand on Noah's shoulder, squeezing gently. "Stay here. The Anderson boy may return and then you can call me on the radio I left you."

31

"You're sure you can't sleep?" Noah asked. He must have heard Kell prowling around, restless. Certainly he hadn't been surprised Kell was making another attempt to find the missing boy; Noah would make a fine cop's boyfriend.

Kell blinked at the strange thought, struggling with a bizarre and inappropriate desire to pull the slighter man into his arms.

"Can't I come with you and help look for him again?" Noah asked calmly.

Kell shook his head reluctantly. "Hiking around your home is one thing, but this might take me into rough country so you'd only slow me down. But... thanks."

Noah was watching him closely and seemed to pick up and accept Kell's resolve. He nodded. "I'll have hot coffee and food waiting whenever you make it back," he offered.

"Thanks." Kell hesitated but then made himself leave Noah and the warm haven of his house behind him.

DEPUTY ALEC DANVERS was on the patio, waiting for the Chief. He was fingering a leather pouch he wore around his neck and looking at the woods speculatively. "Dawn's in another hour; it will be safer to look for the boy then," Alec observed.

"Safer?" Kell cocked a brow at his friend. Alec shook his head, obviously not wanting to share his thoughts.

Kell looked back over his shoulder, meeting Noah's eyes through his kitchen window. "We go now," he said.

WYLDE remembered when his grandfather had been alive, vaguely. He'd lived in the same house then as the boy and the man, except things had been new and in better shape. But then something had happened one night, his grandpa's chest had hurt really bad, and he'd... Wylde had fled into the forest.

He'd lived there ever since, on scraps he found in tin cans outside people's homes or dumpsters in town.

Twice he'd made friends with people, and they'd seemed nice, one giving him his name, Wylde, but then they'd tried to capture him, hurt him.

MORLEY ORRIS parked his truck near the path he used to get to his little greenhouse deep in the woods. Morley had lived all his life at the bottom of Sullivan's Mountain on one branching root of foothill. Early this evening, he'd sat out on his porch and watched the headlights flash past as the men looking for that fool rich boy headed down the mountain to catch some shut-eye before resuming the search.

Probably wouldn't find him anymore than they had those hikers last summer, since it was easy to get turned around up there. Even the lumber companies hadn't had much luck. Morley remembered his father said they'd had some bad luck back in the sixties when they'd shaved slopes of trees in the mess of canyons.

Thanks to being a bit of a night owl, Morley had an idea what all lived on that mountain. He'd even told one other person the secret. The same person he was blackmailing, it turned out.

He didn't especially want to go up the mountain tonight, but he had no choice. His little greenhouse and generator had somehow avoided detection from law enforcement when they looked for the hikers previously, but he couldn't count on it a third time, not unless he used the camouflage tarp he'd rigged up last time. It had worked like a charm.

His stock was all ready to go to his connection in Oregon, and although he had no doubt the Chief had better things to do than bust up his crop of Mary Jane, he'd be duty-bound if he stumbled over it, now wouldn't he? And as lucrative as the blackmail was turning out to be, despite the creepy threats like the dead raccoon whose blood had spelled out "don't push me" that he'd found on his front porch one morning, he didn't want to neglect a sure thing.

Lurching to a stop next to the weedy track he used, Morley didn't want to leave the warm haven of his truck, but he forced himself to open the door, the creak of metal overloud in the watchful silence of the woods.

Almost dawn, he comforted himself. He'd be back in his own bed at dawn, and then he could think of how he would spend his latest windfall.

But as he headed down the path toward his little greenhouse, he was glad that he had his gun, fully loaded, as well as his flashlight.

KELL'S hand went instinctively to the holstered gun on his hip as he studied the shadows. He pushed aside a fir branch with his other hand, heavy with the dew of the deep forest, and scanned the trail ahead.

"Looks like footprints, maybe," he told Alec, pointing to the ground ahead.

Alec nodded, his hand clasping his deerskin bundle. He'd been touching it constantly as they tracked, his face contained. "Looks like Thomas Anderson came this way, headin' toward Morley's land just like you thought. See, Chief?" Alec indicated the larger footprints in the mud, the imprint from some expensive boots that both men figured belonged to young Anderson.

Alec knelt for a closer look and then looked up at Kell, waiting a beat as if to see if he'd grasp the significance. "But there's something else...." He pointed to a soft imprint. "Someone wearing some kind of strange footgear, like leather wrapped around his feet. Seen this before, a time or two. Crude moccasins."

"Yeah, me too," Kell grunted. "But what I want to know is how the hell is the mystery tracker managing to trail Thomas out here in the dark?"

"Might be that this is his... territory," Alec said. "Seems like he knows the forest."

"Well, whateverthefuck. I want to find that boy. Soon!"

Alec gave him a straight look, and they both remembered how they'd searched for Ralph Hindle until they'd found a few red bones and a crushed skull. The hikers, a young couple, they'd never found. The mountains were an unforgiving place.

"Yeah," Alec agreed, climbing back to his feet. "We have to find him soon, before he gets totally lost out here!"

He raced down the path, leaping over mossy fallen logs in the pre-dawn darkness, and Kell didn't waste any time following, the back of his neck clammy with sweat.

Chapter 4

THOMAS ANDERSON covered his mouth, trying to stifle his heavy panting. He was so fucking scared! When he'd thought he'd heard something in the woods with him and Jade, he'd shot at it, but the gun going off had been so loud! And then Jade had started in on him, so he'd shoved her, and then he hadn't heard her again. Had he hurt her? He'd fucking peeled out, trying to get to the house in the woods. Instead, somehow he'd gotten turned around, leaping over rocks, fallen trees, panicked. Worse, for the past few minutes, he'd sensed that something was following *him*. He could feel it, and sometimes he heard a branch snap under a footfall on his trail. Shit! It was the thing that got into their trash, night after night, the thing some called the ghost, he just knew it.

Now he bent over, shaking hand clenched over the stitch in his side, huffing for breath as quietly as he could. His face and body stung with scratches, and his shoulder oozed blood from a puncture wound. Somehow he'd lost his Dad's fucking gun, which was great since the old man was proud of his collection and would have Thomas's ass.

Through his tears, he spotted… light? A light moving through the woods!

Someone was out here with him. Someone with a flashlight. Oh, Christ! Tears stung his eyes in painful relief as he gathered himself, almost played out, moving clumsily through the woods toward the bobbing beacon.

"WAIT...." Alec held up a hand. They paused, listening, looking at each other as they both caught the sounds of something moving through the brush.

"Can you tell where it's coming from?" Kell wiped the sweat from his forehead, and Alec gave him a faintly amused look. "Yeah, been a while since I did regular PT." Kell shrugged. "I'll have to add running again to the workout in my home gym."

Alec pointed to some crushed prints beside the deer trail they were following. "Sounds like it was coming from that rise just ahead, Chief, but this is what I wanted to show you. Another track. This one from what looks like maybe a full grown man."

"That's not the weird moccasin print or one from Thomas Anderson, that's sure," Kell said flatly, feeling a chill prickle down his back.

"Someone else...." Alec said grimly. "A hunter maybe?"

"Come on, we'd better find Thomas!" Kell jogged up the steep incline, grabbing for handholds of roots and granite as he and Alec climbed the next rise.

WYLDE froze on the trail, waiting, barely breathing.

At first he'd been following the other kid, wanting to know where he was going. He was running the way Wylde had once run, deep into the woods, scared. But now he had the sense someone else was out here with them. A hunter trailing them? Wylde usually hid from them.

Light pierced the darkness. Wylde saw it, bouncing off tree trunks and branches in the distance like a dancing fairy from one of his grandpa's stories in the pre-dawn chill.

Someone with a flashlight!

The hunter trailing him must have seen it too; Wylde stiffened as he heard something crash through the underbrush nearby, heading swiftly toward the source of that light.

Still hunting.

"JESUS MURPHY, boy!" Morley Orris lowered his shotgun, recognizing one of his best new customers. "What in the hell are you doin', runnin' at me like that? I nearly plugged you!"

"Please!" Thomas was shivering. He looked over his shoulder. "There's something following me!"

"Yeah, but I doubt he'd mean you any harm," Orris groused, hefting his gun and peering warily into the darkness. "We're closer to my greenhouse than my truck. C'mon, we'll hole up there until it's light. It'll be dawn in a few minutes."

"I don't want to stay here!" Thomas dug his heels in, tugging Orris's arm. "P-please let's go to your truck and get the fuck out of here!"

They both heard something dry snap underfoot in the forest behind them. "Huh, now that's strange; usually he don't come too close to folks," Orris noted. But there was one other possibility, and that definitely gave him a cold chill when he remembered the dead raccoon and the warning before his last push for more money. "C'mon, let's head for my clearing!" He shoved Thomas ahead and trained his shotgun on their back trail. Just his luck the fool boy had come running to him for help. But at least he was someone who could be counted on not to blab about Orris's crop to the Chief.

A branch swayed a few feet behind them, and Orris had a sudden, bad feeling—

"Run, boy!" he yelled.

LEAPING over rocks and fallen logs, gasping for breath, Orris kept the flashlight trained on the ground in front of them. Thomas was in the lead with Orris behind him, one impatient hand shoving him forward as they sprinted for the meadow.

And then they could see the little structure through the woods, Orris's green grow lights casting an eerie beacon, the generator humming, the sound both prosaic and reassuring.

"*Almost there!*" Orris gasped in triumph from behind him. "Door's unlocked, just—"

Thomas snatched the thin plywood door and it creaked open triumphantly. *Safe.* They were—

The flashlight went out. Thomas didn't want to look back, but he couldn't help himself, head turning, looking out of the corner of his eye.

"H-hey, Orris?" he whispered.

Boom! Boom!

He fell back inside the greenhouse, slamming the wooden door shut.

A choked off scream, sound like… wet paper tearing—

Thomas waited, his heart beating in his ears, huddled on the greenhouse floor, hands around his knees. He heard something moving around outside.

"Mister?" he called softly.

Something scratched at the door, as if searching for the latch.

Please… please…. He wasn't sure whom he was begging as he trembled in the darkness.

I'm safe. Nothing's out there. I'm safe. He said the mantra over and over again in his head.

Then the door was thrown open, and he *screamed*—

"*SHIT!*" Kell was over the rise like a big cat. He could see a faint light coming through the trees where the gunshots and the scream had come from—

Alec pulled out his shotgun and ran beside him, eyes wide and dark as he tracked the woods around them.

THEIR feet hit a path only as wide as a single man could run. Kell took point, trusting Alec to get his back since they'd served together in the Rangers. Suddenly, they exploded into a clearing as the sun prickled through the bottom of the trees, lighting the grass and a greenhouse in the center.

Instinctively Kell fell back on training, knowing Alec would also remember. He held up his fist and then made a familiar hand sign: *cover this area.*

Gliding opposite Kell, Alec circled, his eyes showing white as he peered around warily. Kell took the other side, keeping the hut and Alec in his line of vision.

Nothing.

Then Alec gestured, *come.*

Kell sprinted across the meadow to his deputy's side. Alec pointed. More crushed brush, like something had rolled... or been dragged....

Kell knelt, touching one of the leaves. "Blood," he whispered. "Looks like a *lot* of blood...."

"Thomas Anderson? Shit, Chief!" Alec cursed.

There was only one way to find out, Kell knew. Acting in tandem, they made for the greenhouse. While Alec covered him, he raised his leg and kicked the door in.

Both men trained their guns on the greenish-lit interior.

A pale hand lifted, shaking, as if rising from the depths of the ocean, and then a white-faced Thomas Anderson staggered out of the little hut.

Kell's shoulders slumped and his gun fell to his side.

"Boy, I hope you learned a lesson about hiking on your lonesome," he cracked, shaking from the scare, sure he'd lost this kid. He didn't care for Marisa Anderson much, and her husband was coldly removed, barely ever around since he had important business dealings that kept him traveling, but Kell certainly didn't want the teen to come to harm.

He was trembling, so Kell squeezed his shoulder. "You're safe now," he added gruffly.

"It was the ghost. I saw him!" Thomas whispered. He had his arms wrapped around himself, but Kell could see he was only comfortable taking so much reassurance from the men.

Kell shook his head, not buying it. He didn't believe in ghosts, despite the rumors. "Listen, we'll talk about that later, but you didn't happen to shoot a gun in the woods, did you?" Kell prodded.

Thomas dropped his head.

Kell sighed. "Well, I figure your old man is going to be really, *really* pissed at you," he warned the boy. "Where is it, son?"

"Lost it," Thomas mumbled, and for a moment his eyes swam with tears. "Is Jade okay?"

Kell nodded, and Thomas looked desperately relieved.

Alec was still staring into the forest, frowning. "Good thing you found this hut, kid," he commented. "Probably saved you wandering further into the forest and getting totally lost."

Thomas shook his head, looking like he was fighting tears. "No... it wasn't me. Morley Orris helped me. I've seen him around town. He... he...."

"Where is he?" Kell looked around.

Thomas pointed at something lying in the grass in the shadow of the hut. Alec knelt beside it, picking it up. "Flashlight," he said. "Still on."

Thomas scrubbed his eyes as if embarrassed as more tears fell. "I heard him shoot at something and then nothing." The teen covered his face, and Kell could see he was too far gone to say more.

"Stay here a minute." Kell left Thomas and strode over to the meadow edge where the crushed bushes were. He dug around, frowning, before he lifted an abandoned shotgun up with one finger.

He looked over at Alec and Thomas before turning and studying the flattened brush again, wondering. Just what the hell had gone on in the forest tonight?

"I think the ghost got him," Thomas breathed.

"HEY," Kell said, feeling a warm glow as he walked into Noah Matthews's sixties kitchen, which was half-renovated. The sun was high over the trees now, and the blue sky and sunshine sparkled on the Matthews's pool, forgiving of the unnatural shade of purple.

Noah studied him. "You okay?"

Kell nodded, feeling strange. When was the last time anyone had cared?

"You found the boy," Noah added. "Josh and I heard...."

Kell said, "He shouldn't have gone out there and I think he knows it now. Unfortunately for him, his old man was around from one of his business trips, so he's giving him hell."

Noah challenged Kell with a look from serious gray eyes. "I can't say I blame him. If it had been Josh.... I'd not want him ever going in those woods, risking getting lost," he said quietly, but nevertheless, Kell caught the whiff of disapproval: *back off, you are not a parent.*

Kell rubbed his tight neck. Fair enough—he was no one's daddy. And anyway, he had to go talk to Thomas Anderson's parents once they calmed down. Then he and his men were going back to the woods to see if they could find Morley Orris. So far all they'd discovered were his abandoned truck and some traces that something heavy had been dragged from the meadow, but that was it. The local pot farmer had disappeared.

Or something got him.

Kell suppressed the thought. He wasn't a fanciful man. He believed in hard facts. They'd investigate and find Orris. Besides, he'd thought for years the ghost story was bogus. It seemed that it was always stealing food, going through garbage. In other words, it ate, which didn't seem otherworldly to Kell.

"Chief... Kell," Noah interrupted his thoughts. "Stay for breakfast."

Kell felt his heart speed up a little at the invitation. He smiled, noticing that Noah's gray eyes had softened. He put his hat down and watched as Noah opened the fridge and pulled out an unappetizing white slab of something that jiggled on a plate.

Kell frowned at it. Shit, where were the eggs and bacon?

"Scrambled tofu coming up. Would you also like a glass of organic wheat grass juice?" Noah asked him calmly.

Kell blinked. "You've got to be fucking kidding me!"

Noah grinned, raising a pale brow, his ash-blond hair tangled around his unshaven face.

"You're going to be a handful," Kell predicted, his tone caressing.

HOURS later, Kell cut through the Matthews's yard to return to his SUV. He was sweaty and hot and limping because he'd tripped on some deadfall and nearly taken an embarrassing tumble in front of his men.

In short, he was in a piss-poor mood.

In cool contrast, Noah Matthews climbed out of the pool, his body as perfect as a classical marble statue.

Kell came to a halt, staring, his weariness forgotten as he watched the graceful, slender figure pick up a towel and dry his slick chest. He suppressed a groan, but just barely. He wanted to *lick* the droplets of water running over sleek, softly defined muscles. Take Noah's water-dark hair in a fist and hold his head steady as he captured his mouth in a fierce, possessive kiss—

He blinked.

He guessed he probably *was* a barbarian for having such thoughts about a man innocently taking a swim. And anyway, he had the feeling Noah would require careful handling. He'd certainly told Kell off for being judgmental of a parent's concerns. Was Kell up for that? Hell yes, his gut answered.

"Did you find that poor man?"

Kell shook his head, a little chagrined at his intense thoughts.

Noah stopped him with a gentle hand on his sleeve. "You look done in. That guest room is yours if you need it, even if the house is…." Noah sighed, shrugging.

"It's not purple, is it?" Kell asked, nodding toward the pool.

"Nope." Shy warmth glimmered in Noah's eyes.

Kell rubbed the back of his tight neck. "Don't flirt with me if you don't mean it, Noah. I don't play games."

Noah's eyes widened. "I meant it as a kindness, not a—"

Kell raised a hand, cutting him off. "I know, I'm sorry. I'm a bit… down to earth."

"You're a caveman, Chief," Noah corrected wryly. But he smiled, and that smile made Kell's pulse race.

"Okay, I'd appreciate that. But I don't have to drink anymore of that grass shit, right?"

NOAH made up the bed with fresh sheets while Kell showered. He came out of the bathroom wearing a large towel around his waist and felt his throat tighten for some goddamned stupid reason, watching Noah ensuring the comfort of his guest.

He reminded himself he just wanted a hot, fast lay, and he had no room in his solitary life for anything else.

"You're staring at my ass," Noah said primly, straightening to glare at Kell.

"I'd like to spend about an hour nibbling on it, so just be glad all I do is stare," Kell said, unrepentant. He couldn't believe how fast he heated up whenever he was around Noah.

His cheeks flushed—he told himself he was warm from the shower, *not* blushing like a green kid—as he quickly dropped the towel and, ignoring Noah's interested gaze, climbed swiftly into the newly made bed, hiding his impressive woody safely under the covers. He cleared his throat before saying sincerely, "This is... nice. Thank you."

Noah swallowed. "No, thank *you*, Chief. I'm glad you found that kid so that Josh and I can get on with our first few days here, argue about watching *300*."

"Hear there's some nice homoerotic subtext in that flick." Kell quirked a brow, baiting Noah.

Noah's answer was a tossed cushion thrown Kell's way before he closed the door behind him.

Kell grinned, rolling over onto his stomach, luxuriating in the comfortable bed, exhausted. "He likes me, I know it," he whispered before drifting to sleep.

Chapter 5

KELL was dreaming. He even knew he was dreaming on some level, shifting on the cool, fresh sheets of Noah's guest bed restlessly, his hands opening and closing into fists.

He was back in the woods. Hungry, cold. He was lying under a rotting tree trunk, eyes open in the darkness, thinking of the people living so close by, warm, safe.

Most of all, he was scared. Scared of the woman who at first had seemed so nice, leaving him food, but then the man had chased him away one day when he'd caught a glimpse of him.

And there was the greenhouse in the woods, glowing light.

He went there sometimes, watched the man tending the plants.

"Kell!"

Kell blinked, wide eyes snapping open to fix on Noah. He was sitting up in bed, the sheets tumbled down to his lap. His face and chest were slick with sweat. He was gripping Noah's forearms, and as he came back to himself, gasping for breath, he belatedly realized his grip was hard enough to leave bruises on Noah's skin.

"Shit! I'm... sorry," he whispered, dropping his hands and falling back against the headboard, still trembling. Great, here was the man he wanted to lure into his bed—and he'd done it, but in a way Kell had never wanted. He didn't like appearing vulnerable to anyone.

46

"I could hear you from my study! Are you all right?" Noah's gray eyes were warm and concerned.

Unused to anyone looking at him that way, Kell nodded, swallowing thickly. He closed his eyes, scrubbing shaking fingers over his slick face.

The bed creaked as Noah got up and went to the en suite. He reappeared with water in a glass tumbler, handing it calmly to Kell.

Kell gulped down the water and then rubbed the cool glass against his forehead.

"You had some kind of bad dream?" Noah probed.

Kell shrugged, not wanting to share the nightmare. Even now it was fading into scattered impressions, like leaves blown by a fall wind. He scratched his bare chest and saw Noah's gaze fall to his skin.

Now *this* he understood and welcomed.

His adrenaline still pumping from the dream, Kell put down the glass and snagged Noah's slender wrist, pulling him onto the side of the bed.

Noah began, hands raised, "Kell...."

Kell took in wide gray eyes and a scattering of freckles on Noah's pale skin before he cupped the other man's cheeks and pulled him into a kiss. "I'm not someone you have to take care of," he murmured.

"Is it so wrong to let someone take care of you?" Noah frowned.

Kell didn't want to talk. He had Noah where he wanted him now, and discussing his brief vulnerability was not something he wanted to do. What he did want.... He nipped Noah's lush bottom lip so when the other man gasped in shock, he put his tongue inside Noah, groaning at the burning rightness of penetrating him.

"You want me in you," Kell growled, triumphant. "Baby, I can feel it!"

His hands were in Noah's curls, holding his head as he loved him with his tongue, stroking it voluptuously over Noah's timid one, drinking in the soft sound Noah gave, showing him just how fucking good it could be—

Abruptly Noah struggled, and Kell released him, a satisfied smile touching his lips as the slighter man ran an unsteady hand through the curls that Kell had mussed while he'd claimed Noah's mouth.

"You can't just grab me and kiss me like some kind of goddamned wild man!" Noah stated, looking pissy. The soft, cloudy look that he'd worn directly after Kell had kissed him cleared, and the familiar snap was back in his affronted gray eyes.

"Wild man, huh?" Kell bit his lips before continuing, focusing on Noah. "Baby," Kell said in a deep, husky voice, his erection throbbing hungrily under the sheets, "I'm sorry if I scared you. I just had to be inside you."

Noah jumped off the bed. "I told you I wasn't—"

Kell raised a hand, getting pissy himself. "You rang my gaydar from the minute I met you, so don't give me that shit."

"My… reticence is *not* shit! And I also don't appreciate being manhandled. When I date someone, I expect things to be… different."

Kell could see his eyes take on a familiar predatory gleam in the mirror opposite the bed. He carefully veiled them from Noah with his eyelashes, since he was already in hot water. "So what do you expect when you date someone?"

"I…." Noah looked thrown for a moment by Kell's calm question, but then his mouth tightened. "Well… we might attend social functions together. Visit the theater. Go to an art gallery viewing. We'd eat together. Talk about books we've read and places we've traveled."

Kell chewed his lip. "Huh. Last thing I read was *Lightning* by Dean Koontz. Places I've traveled I'm still not allowed to talk about. The only theater in town is at the high school. But I could take you to a movie and for a meal at the diner."

Noah huffed out a disbelieving laugh. "You're actually asking me out on a date? Are you for real?"

"Yep," Kell said.

"Kell, I will not play Jane to your Tarzan!"

Kell smiled. "I don't want Jane. I want you."

"Dad, how come you're growling at the Chief?" Josh interrupted, walking in and rubbing sleepy eyes. Bright late afternoon sunlight illuminated his tousled hair as he looked from one man to the other, as if feeling the tension pulsing between them.

Noah swallowed, giving Kell a warning look.

Kell's mouth flattened in a grim line. Did Noah think he was going to push the come-on with a kid in the room? He sat on his temper, knowing he'd have to show who he was to the wary Noah. "Your dad was just a little pissed at me for something I did," Kell told Josh. "How are you feeling? I guess this isn't the way you imagined moving in would be."

"OKAY, I guess," Josh said. He noticed his dad was flushed and avoiding his gaze. Of course, he'd heard the whole thing: the Chief wanted to date his dad, and his dad was freaking out. He guessed he had to act like a total kid and pretend he didn't know what was going on or Noah would probably pass out.

At school in Seattle, Josh's older best friend had been gay. That was not a big deal. But since it was his dad…. It wasn't that the

Chief was male exactly, it was…. Josh sighed, not sure how he was feeling but embarrassed it might be kind of like a little kid or something, accustomed to having Noah's attention focused solely on him.

"So, someone made off with some food, your Dad tells me." Kell's questioning voice broke into Josh's thoughts.

Comfortable with the Chief despite his gruffness, Josh sat down on the corner of the guest bed and put aside his qualms. "Yeah, it was weird. Like, most of our dinner. But it has to be someone who needed it more, right? At least that's what I think," he said gravely. "It wasn't that kid Thomas, was it?"

"Nope, not him. Just do me a favor and don't take any hikes in the woods for a while. I think…." The Chief scrubbed his unshaven jaw, and Josh could almost read his thoughts; he didn't want to scare the city kid. "There's maybe a bear… or, uh, something in the woods."

Or something, Josh thought. "I'll stay around the house. So the Chief is going to take us to a movie? Can we see something cool?"

KELL didn't miss how Noah's eyes widened. *Trapped!*

He laughed, enjoying that Noah would probably have to go out with him after all, and he actually didn't mind Josh coming with them. "Sure, I'll take you both out tonight, but your Dad has final say on the movie choice."

Josh rolled his eyes. "Just please tell me it won't be Disney, okay? I'm not a total kid!"

AT THE diner, Jade refreshed Alec's coffee as he leaned back in his chair. He looked tired, she noticed as he nodded courteously toward her, though his flushed cheeks gave him away; He was still sweet on her. He'd been sweet on her forever, but Jade didn't want to run him over in one of her drive-by affairs. He was a nice kid, maybe seven years younger than herself. Nicely shaped too, ever since he'd been in the Rangers.

Alec cleared his throat. "Say, Jade, I thought you'd be at home, resting."

"Can't afford to lie around, and it was embarrassing the other night, being carted off in an ambulance," she said. "I'm just glad that Thomas is okay. His mother fired me." Jade raised a brow.

"I'm sorry, but you can't blame her." Alec shook his head. "Even if she seems a bit of a difficult woman."

"And why is that?" Jade asked in an imperious tone.

"Because a woman like you around her little boy? Nuh uh. The woman and her husband are total control freaks, Jade."

"I'll have you know, I'd never have…!"

Alec raised a hand. "Hey, I know. I've been… I've known you since I was fifteen, remember? She just doesn't know that you're a good person as well as beautiful."

Jade cleared her throat, rubbing the bruise on her forehead self-consciously. "Yeah, right." Knowing he was going to ask her out, she let a little coffee splatter, buying some time because she wasn't sure exactly what her answer would be. "Oh crap!" she cursed loudly, making heads turn in shock. Well, let Alec see her for who she was, and that wasn't goddamned Doris Day, now was it? "Sorry about that!"

"It's okay. You didn't get me," Alec said. A wry look came into his soft chocolate eyes, as if he knew what she was up to, cutting him off before he could make a move. Huh.

She turned her back, deciding that even if *she* didn't want him, there was no harm in him wanting her, so she rolled her hips as she headed to the counter for paper towels to clean up her mess. But

51

when she looked over her shoulder, sure he'd be staring at her lush ass like every other man in this hick town, she saw with surprise he was looking into her eyes gravely.

He stood up, took his hat and nodded to her politely before quietly leaving.

"Well, damn!" Jade was abruptly irritated. Why did he have to do something that would make her think about him and wonder? The only other man immune to her attractions was the Chief, and wasn't *that* a waste, since he was such a honey.

"You're nothin' special, Alec Danvers," Jade muttered, slamming the coffee back down on its warmer.

IT WAS just after dark when she got in her beloved jeep and headed for the foothills where she lived. Her house was about a mile from that missing pot farmer's, Morley Orris. Truth be told, she kind of missed him living there, even though he had a habit of lurking and nosing into people's private stuff. Jade always figured that was an unhealthy trait, with all the secrets in her small town, people fooling around on the side, but for her part she had none, so Morley didn't threaten her. And with him missing, no one lived on the lonely dead-end road at the foot of the mountain but Jade.

But of course she wasn't afraid or anything. Folks talked about some ghost on the mountain, but that was all just bull. She'd been hearing campfire stories since she was a girl. She knew truth from fiction, and despite the upsetting experience she'd had the other night, she was convinced the only things up that mountain were wild animals and too much fresh air. Too bad Thomas hadn't seen that before he'd used his father's gun and then almost gotten himself seriously lost.

She was on the last curve of road leading to her house when her jeep sputtered and died.

"Well, son of a *bitch!*" She got out and opened the hood, seeing steam coming from the engine. It could be any number of things. Her jeep was always breaking down, but she didn't have the money to fix it.

She growled to herself, realizing she'd have to walk to her house. Damn it, her feet were sore from working all day, and her head was pounding from the knock she'd taken in the woods. Alec had been right to be surprised to see her working again so soon; she really should have taken a day off, she guessed.

She let her head fall back and briefly imagined Alec Danvers coming to her rescue in his air-conditioned SUV. She snorted at the picture. "You are never going to be Cinderella, honey, so you walk," she scolded herself.

Not seeing any point in putting it off, she slammed the door of her jeep closed, making sure it was locked up. Her feet hurt so much, she thought about taking her shoes off and walking barefoot, but the asphalt was old, like walking on hot pebbles, so she left them on. The faster she got walking, the sooner she got home—not that anyone was waiting for her, but that was the way she liked it, she reminded herself, irritated when she had another vision of Alec's eyes on her face. She was doing him a favor, not taking him for a one-nighter. Those heartbroken eyes told her he wasn't the type.

Something snapped in the woods that ran alongside the road, and her heart gave a little bump. She paused, listening, but heard nothing more. It was very quiet.

"Naw, nothing to worry about, girl," she scolded herself. This wasn't a repeat of the other night, not that she remembered much, other than hitting her head suddenly.

She lifted her bag higher on her shoulder and continued heading down the road to her TV and a mac and cheese dinner, or maybe Thai with noodles tonight.

About a half mile from her car, she looked back over her shoulder and saw a branch swaying by the road. There was no wind to speak of, so she felt a cold chill poke her spine. "There's nothing there!" she muttered. "Don't be an idiot, Jade." She'd lived here for years and never seen anything much, except sometimes something got in her garbage, but that was to be expected up here.

Still, she picked up her pace, almost running now on the road leading to her darkened house. She could just make out the roof peeking out of the bottom of the tall trees surrounding it.

Behind her, something crashed through the brush—

Chapter 6

JADE was running, her breath making little frantic sobs as she raced for her home, forgetting dignity now. Behind her, she could hear the crash of something chasing her through the strip of woods that paralleled the lonely road.

Suddenly she caught the sound of hard footfalls on tarmac.

This isn't happening, this is bullshit! Anger flared, saving her.

Heart thundering, she dug frantically in her bag, grabbing what she needed and dropping the bag, spinning around—

"Get back, fucker, or I'll waste you!" Jade yelled, pointing her gun at her pursuer.

"You'd shoot a peace officer, Jade?" Alec asked, hands up. He was huffing, color bright at the top of his cheeks.

"*Holy...!*" Jade dropped the gun to her side and then paced, muttering to herself. "Turnip brain! Dickwad!"

"Hey, now, no need to be impolite. You okay?" Alec gently took the gun from her shaking hand, checking it out in experienced hands. "Beretta 92. Eight and a half inches long. Big gun for a woman to carry," he noted mildly.

"Give it back!" Jade spat, getting her wind back. "Pumpkin brain!"

Alec's eyes widened, but instead of being pissed or offended, he looked amused. He had a cut across his cheek, Jade noted, from what looked like whiplash from a branch.

"Why the hell were you stalkin' me?"

"I'm part of the search party looking for Morley. I was tracking something and I heard you running. Thought you were the ghos—er, hope I didn't scare you."

Jade laughed, heart still pounding, but she was damned if she'd let him see that. "Scare me? *You?*" She looked him up and down, pretending contempt but taking in his rumpled uniform and the way the muscles in his forearms flexed as he unchambered her weapon and gave it back to her. "Oh good. At least you're not stupid enough to disarm the little woman. That always drives me nuts in horror movies."

Alec grinned, and Jade was caught for a second by his dark good looks under the faint light of a distant street lamp. His face was angular, olive-toned, not a looker at first glance, until you were caught in the reflection of simmering chocolate eyes. "Honey, you have weapons a man should be wary of even without the gun. You got a permit to carry that, right?"

"Yeah, sure," Jade lied.

Alec scratched the back of his neck, looking as if he didn't quite believe her and knew that he was not batting a thousand with Jade but wasn't sure he cared. Instead, he had the air of man who simply appreciated. Huh. He was a piece of work, but no way was she letting him under her skin.

"Just don't shoot any county deputies and we'll forget it. I actually feel better knowing you got that little cannon. You really should move closer to town," he suggested, putting a protective hand on her arm, his callused fingertips making her want to shiver from a weird intensity sparking from his touch.

Jade shook him off to get down and pick up the scattered debris from her bag. Alec also knelt to help her patiently. He didn't even blush when he handed her a Kotex box. Being in the Rangers had sure changed him.

"I like it up here. It's my land and no spooky bullshit is going to drive me away, you hear?"

"Yes, ma'am." Alec smiled before asking wistfully, "Do you like living alone? I don't."

She shrugged, letting him walk her home. "Yeah, it's fine. Not like I'm dying to pick up after some man."

"Some men pick up after themselves, Jade." Alec frowned. "And how come you're on foot? The jeep went again?"

"Yeah. I'll go out and fix it in the morning." Jade was pretty handy now, caring for her beloved jeep. She took pride in the fact that only rarely did she have to take it to the shop.

"If you got some tools, I can tow it to your house for you and give you a hand."

"I can take care of it myself." She pressed her lips together, uncomfortable with the idea she'd owe him or anyone else any favors.

"Never hurts to let a friend help you."

"You just want to get in my pants!" she scoffed.

Alec blinked, but again he didn't blush. Well, damn. His confidence was getting on her nerves. Did nothing shake him? She knew he wanted her. He'd *always* wanted her, from the time he was fifteen.

"Sure I do. Who wouldn't? You're a beautiful woman, Jade, but I'd rather be your friend first," Alec retorted, somewhat primly.

Jade gave a bitter sound, pulling out the fixings for a cigarette as they walked. The woods that had seemed so menacing minutes before now gave her a familiar sense of sanctuary. She lived up here so she could feel alone. So she wouldn't ever lean too hard on someone and fall on her ass when they let her down. "I don't fuck my friends."

"Exactly." He smiled, white teeth gleaming in his tanned face. "I was thinking more about making love, myself."

57

She nearly dropped her cigarette but settled for raising a dark brow. "Guys don't think that way."

"This guy does. And that's a stereotype, anyway."

"Yeah, whatever." Jade lit up and saw him eying her cigarette with distaste. "Gonna tell me smoking's bad for my health, good boy?"

"I'm a good boy?" Alec looked amused, attractive crow's feet crinkling beside his dark eyes. "And I try never to state the obvious."

"I noticed," Jade growled, blowing smoke in his direction in more ways than one. "Yeah, you're the good boy and I'm the—"

"You're Jade," Alec interrupted her, as if not even *she* was allowed to insult herself.

"Just remember, I didn't need to be rescued." It was important to point that out, if only for pride's sake. But pride was a lot, for Jade. It had sometimes been all she had.

Alec only smiled, deflecting her annoyance. "Sure, Jade."

FRESHLY showered and dressed, Kell's eyes hungrily tracked Noah as the slighter man followed him out to his truck.

"Sorry about the movie. Lawman's hours." Kell scrubbed his face, feeling the rasp of his growing beard. "I was going to rejoin the search party still lookin' for Morley but I want to swing by and talk to Jade Moreton and see what she remembers. Might give me some ideas on what I'm dealing with."

"I'm glad that girl will be okay," Noah said soberly. "Tell her whenever she feels up to it, we'd appreciate it if she put in some hours at our house. I heard she lost her job over at the Anderson's."

Kell nodded.

"Kell…." Noah hesitated but finally continued, "Do you think it's safe here?" Noah looked at the towering trees rising by his driveway. "I admit that I'm a little uneasy; it wasn't the housewarming I'd expected, looked forward to all these months."

Kell didn't know what to say. "I don't have all the facts but so far the only people that have gone missing or been hurt have been *in* the woods. Just stay out of them and you and Josh should be okay."

Noah took off his glasses, his ash-blond hair mussed. In that moment, he looked as boyish as Josh, which roused Kell's protective instincts. "Thank you for that. I'm glad you didn't try to scare the city boy."

"I think I've scared you enough," Kell said, a little disappointed. Damn, Noah had ducked any chance for a second kiss, and Kell sure wanted one.

"I didn't appreciate how you used Josh to try to twist me into a date," Noah stated, eyes igniting like the blue flame of a lighter. "I've never had the chance to talk to him about… things."

"Things? You mean the fact you're gay," Kell said flatly, giving Noah a direct look, daring him to deny it.

"Yes," Noah confessed softly. "Yes, I've always had these feelings but when I got Margaret pregnant with Josh at a drunken college party, I tried to put it aside, be a good husband."

Kell's jaw tightened. "It wasn't easy for me in the army. Finally had to leave because I couldn't be who I am. And this town… you'd think people would never have voted for me, but folks seemed to like the job I did as a deputy in the area, so…."

"Sounds like there are some smart folks out here in the boonies," Noah said. "They see you for who you are, not where you like to spill your sperm." He lifted a brow as he teased Kell with his own words.

"Some," Kell agreed. He leaned against his truck and let his head fall back. "Although I admit that I'll use any edge I can, just to get to you; I just really wanted to take you and Josh out."

"Josh as well?" Noah looked skeptical. "People have tried to date me by kissing up to my son before."

"People? Sounds like you mean someone in particular," Kell noted.

Noah looked away, mouth tight.

After a telling pause, Kell continued, "Do you think I'm the kind of man for that sort of fancy-ass play?" He regarded Noah calmly.

"No," Noah said. "But you didn't ask before you kissed me."

Kell shrugged. "I'm not sorry, baby."

"What kind of relationship do you see between us?"

Kell blinked. *Relationship?* Uh...."

"What kind of men do you usually date?" Noah looked like he was enjoying getting his claws into Kell. Kell decided he liked it too. *Tiger, just wait until we get close.*

"I don't *date.* I drive two towns over, go to a club, pick someone up and—" He shrugged, doubting prim Noah would want to hear about handcuffs, blow jobs in his SUV, a little rough play.

Noah's hands clenched into fists. He swallowed. "I have a son. He's everything to me. I've built my own career and a stable life, all so I could be a good father. I don't have room in my life for... flings."

Kell raked a hand through his hair. "You don't fit," he agreed crankily.

"Oh, whatever will I do?" Noah said sarcastically. "I'm so sorry I'm not like some floozy you pick up at a bar!"

Kell reached out and cupped the back of Noah's neck, brows lowered. Noah gave a little gasp at his touch, and his pupils dilated. Kell felt himself swell and wished he could rub himself off on that cool, lean body.

"Floozy?" Kell was amused by Noah's quaint talk. "Just horny men looking for some relief. I know what you're scared of, baby," he whispered.

"Really?" Noah's eyes were snapping again like gasoline set alight. "And don't call me 'baby'."

"*Penetration.* You haven't had anyone inside you before and you're scared of taking me."

Noah smacked Kell's hand away. "I'm not scared. I'm pissed off, you barbarian!"

"I promise I'd take care of you."

Noah stared into dark predatory eyes, soft and heated, making promises of sweaty skin against skin and hands fisted in the sheets. He could almost picture Kell on top of him, Noah's legs spread, clutching Kell's working ass—

Whatever he was going to say was interrupted by the urgent squawk of Kell's radio.

"I THOUGHT you had a dog," Alec said as they got closer to Jade's place. He was looking around as if appreciating the touches she'd made, like planting winter pansies near the road so they glimmered in dark violet dots below tall trees.

"Yeah." She frowned. "Beau. He's a retriever I got from the pound. He's old, but he usually barks whenever he hears me come home."

Alec looked around, taking in the unnatural stillness. "Jade, stay here. I want to take a look first."

"Fuck that! That's my dog and my land!" She pulled out her gun and fed in fresh ammunition.

"Just don't shoot me." Alec didn't try to dissuade her, however. The deerskin pouch against his neck was hot, burning a warning as it had earlier when he'd been tracking in the forest.

"Where do you keep your dog when you aren't home?"

"Got a nice house out front I built him myself. He likes to stay outdoors while I'm at work. How come?"

Alec pressed a hand against Jade's shoulder, looking at her gravely. "I know you're tough, but I need you to trust me and let me take a look first, okay? This is what I was trained to do."

"Alec...." She bit her lip and did something she never did, studying his earnest chocolate eyes: she gave in.

He melted into the deep pools of shadow from the trees on her front yard, and Jade stood in the dark, gripping her gun and feeling the seconds tick by in the rapid pounding of her heart.

ALEC stole closer to Jade's house, nose suddenly wrinkling from the smell... like ripe meat....

He looked around for Jade's dog but saw nothing. He tried her front door and was relieved it was locked, so he moved on to peer in her living room window but caught no sign of her pet indoors.

His shoulder blades were itching, telling him there was something bad out here, something he'd missed.

And then he saw it when he swung around to return to Jade.

Hanging from a tree, just like a hide drying, milky eyes wide with terror.

He gagged and lowered his gaze, looking around sharply, but now the deerskin bundle was cooling. Whoever had been here was gone.

But they had left something behind.

Chapter 7

DANIEL MAKEPEACE, the county coroner, stared up at the hanging corpse, raising a reddish-blond brow over contemplative gray eyes. "So guess you found Morley, huh?" he drawled.

Kell felt the burn of personal failure, though he knew it was irrational. But damn it, this was *his* town, and people were getting hurt. And worse, he kept seeing Noah's face when he asked Kell if he thought it was safe.

Kell wanted to make it safe, for Noah, for Josh.

"I need to know who killed him, Daniel," he said quietly, taking his hat off and wiping the sweat from his forehead. "It looks like an animal but…?" Unease moved through his broad shoulders. He'd spent a fair bit of time in woods, in jungles, hunting animals, hunting men. There was something wrong here.

"But why just the skin and bones left like that… and the legs?" one of the deputies demanded. He'd finished puking in Jade's rose bushes and was avoiding looking at the hanging ruin.

"Oh, that's simple," Daniel said, suddenly enthusiastic. "Presumably whatever took him removed all the best parts: heart, lungs, and all the juicy organs. Yum yum! Good eats."

"Jesus, Daniel!" The deputy grimaced, looking like he'd like to visit the bushes again.

"So it was done to resemble a kill for food?" Kell said, hands worrying his hat.

"Yep, done by a very sophisticated animal, Kell." Daniel's lips twisted. "I'd say a skillful hunter who knew just how to butcher Morley efficiently. Slit him open here"—Daniel pointed to Morley's throat. "And all the way down. Cracked open the ribs and clawed out the goodies." He bent closer, plastic gloved hands touching one red-stained rib. "Left the legs and arms virtually intact. Huh, but there is some odd scoring of the bones; I'm not sure what cut him, looks like a primitive kind of knife. I'll have a better idea when I do the post-mortem."

"But why bring Morley down here and peg him up on a sharp branch?" Kell demanded, his back itching like ants were crawling over his skin.

"*Scarecrow....*" Alec muttered. "Maybe it was a warning to someone, an assertion of territory."

Kell turned to Alec, brows lowered, and waited, giving him time. He'd learned to trust his friend's instincts, which were a little unconventional but pretty on the money.

"I mean... Chief, when I first saw Morley, I was reminded in old times people used to hang up wolves' skulls as a warning. *Keep out. This is my place.*"

"A warning...?" Kell crushed his hat under frustrated hands. "Someone warning us to stay out of the woods? Naw, this feels less nebulous, more personal...."

Daniel climbed down Jade's borrowed ladder. "The scoring suggests some kind of handmade blade."

"So no way it was an animal kill that someone just... found and strung up here."

"I think an animal would have finished eating Morley. There's some good protein and fat left on the limbs. Only thing I can tell you for sure is this is an efficient and experienced killer." Daniel removed his gloves with a decisive snap. "Look like you boys got yourselves a problem."

Jade marched out, smoking. She showed no sign that Morley's corpse bothered her, though Alec had seen her face turn white when she'd first insisted on seeing what all was in her front yard.

"Any sign of Beau?" she asked Alec in a subdued tone, dark eyes clouded with weariness… and worry.

Alec shook his head. He offered softly, "I'll go lookin' for him after."

Kell gave Alec a sharp look. "Don't go alone. I want everyone going into the woods in pairs from now on."

Alec hesitated, holding Kell's gaze, but then nodded.

"So then I'll go with you," Jade offered.

"Jade…." Alec looked so unhappy that Kell felt a spike of bleak amusement. Alec had been in love with Jade forever, and everyone knew it, including Jade. Poor man, holding feelings for her was like grabbing a cat by the tail.

"I'm not afraid!" she burst out, looking pissed.

Alec raised a brow.

"Okay, I *am*, but damn it, this is *my* place and… and I want my dog back. He's old, but I'm used to him." Jade pursed her lips, looking away as the deputies helped the coroner take down the body from the tree in her yard. "Alec, please, I just want to find my dog."

Alec nodded, reaching out to squeeze Jade's shoulder. "He's company, I get that."

"Yeah, company," Jade said, swallowing thickly. "I'll be in my kitchen when you're ready."

KELL followed Daniel to his SUV, Alec beside him. "This killer butchered Morley." He swallowed, a little sick. "Do you think he or she… ate him?"

Daniel shrugged, looking grim. "I have no idea, but it does look like a butchered kill and given Morley was placed like a bulletin board in Jade's garden, I think it's a hunter who had an agenda. There's only one predator I know of that is capable of that kind of deliberate action."

"Yeah, *us*." Kell took a deep breath. "I guess this is better, knowing that it's a hunter out there and we need to catch him." So why were his guts twisting like cold snakes, warning him there was more going on here? He looked at Alec. "We need to find out if anyone had it in for Morley, any of his connections for his part-time business, anyone whose wife he might have slept with...."

"Kell...." Daniel hesitated. "Someone has been stealing food from people's homes for years. You know it and I know it."

Kell rubbed the stiff back of his neck. "Yeah. So you're saying the so-called ghost killed Morley?"

"I don't know, but someone certainly wanted to make it look that way... which will probably make folks in town very spooked."

"Shit!" Kell could imagine. He hoped no one shot at his neighbor getting a newspaper or something. And whoever the ghost was, he or she had better stay hidden deep in the woods for a while... as long as they weren't responsible for Morley—because if they were, Kell would come hunting.

JADE MORETON'S kitchen had a dozen red roses seated in a jam jar. Kell could figure out who had sent her the flowers without reading the card, but it struck him as sad that the woman didn't even own a flower vase. Maybe Alec would be good for her, if he could get close enough through the thorns that guarded the rose.

He was briefly amused by the romantic turn of his own thoughts, but maybe he had a reason lately to be feeling that way, and it beat hell out of thinking about gory hanging bodies. Still, he had to get his mind back to the business at hand. "Jade," Kell greeted the waitress, sitting down in the offered chair.

"Chief," she rasped. "I was thinking of getting very drunk. Want to join me?" She pulled a bottle of Johnnie Walker out of the cupboard.

"I'm on duty," Kell sighed with some regret. "Guess you know what I'm here for."

She nodded.

"Nice flowers," he said, seeking to put her at her ease.

"Yeah, Alec, you know...."

"I do." Kell's gaze sharpened. "I need to know what you remember from the night you and Thomas got lost in the forest." He pulled out a notebook. "You headed up the trail for a swim in Noah Matthews's pool, is that right?"

"Yep. From my conversations with Noah, he seems a good guy, really crazy about his kid. He was gentlemanly enough to say it would be all right for me to use the pool sometimes and... I guess I'm comfortable about that since it's not too fancy, you know. Plus, his pool has the power of purple working for it." Jade's eyes were briefly amused as she gave a shrug, and Kell remembered that, like him, she was a foster kid, raised by a divorced mother here in town; it figured Noah's parenting would impress her. "I don't remember much. That kid Thomas thought he heard a sound, he fired his Dad's gun at something and then he shoved me... next thing I had a hell of a headache."

Kell eyed her bruise. "You really should have taken work off."

"Don't kid a kidder. You would have done the same as me," Jade observed, reaching for a fresh cigarette. "And I'm determined not to be sidetracked from my life or driven away from my home."

"Uh huh." Kell felt some sympathy for Alec at her independent attitude. And yet, wasn't Noah the same way?

JOSH stared out at the woods, his brow furrowed.

He'd been wondering about whoever had stolen their food, worrying that maybe the person was hungry, cold out there....

"Josh?" His dad put a hand on his shoulder. "Come away from the window. I thought we'd look at that Sheltie magazine again."

Josh nodded. His dad was treating the decision to get a dog like everything he did, cautiously. He insisted they both read up on breeds and discuss what might suit their new lifestyle, but it was kind of nifty to discuss their first choice. Josh knew he was lucky in the way Noah included him in all their decisions, which also made it important he let his dad know something....

"It's okay if you're gay, Dad," Josh blurted.

Noah blinked before color suffused his cheeks. "Josh...."

"I mean, uh, I guess *bi* is more the correct term, seeing as you had me, so you had to like Mom's body. But I'm just saying if you like penises, I'm okay with that." He had to do this for his Dad. He'd been practically a shut-in for several months back in Seattle before they'd moved, and Josh had the idea his previous friendship with another man might have had something to do with it.

Noah went to the kitchen table and sat down, running a hand over his face. He looked totally freaked out. "This is about the Chief."

"I like him. Okay, I admit the gay thing is slightly, uh. Do you think I'll be...?"

"Josh, I have no idea, but I'll love you whoever you are," Noah said firmly. Then he took a deep breath and leaped off a cliff with his kid. "Can you do the same for me?"

"I'll try." Josh blew out a breath. "He won't mean that you... don't have as much time for me?"

Noah frowned. "I don't know," he answered, trying to be honest with his son as always. "Maybe a tiny bit less because if I date someone, I might enjoy a little time with him, and I know that might be hard, since it's just been us for a long time."

Josh finally confessed, "I don't know how I feel about this. I mean, I want to be all adult and shit but—"

"It's okay. I know it has to be...." Noah shrugged. "I also know you like him. He's a good man." Noah covered his eyes. "I can't believe we're discussing this."

"Hey, you're the one who told me about safe sex and condoms way before the school nurse." Josh raised his hands.

Noah nodded. "All right. We're two men here...." He cleared his throat. "Wouldn't you rather talk about Shetland Sheepdogs? There is that rescue site we found online...."

"Sorry, Dad, you're so not off the hook!" Josh pulled out a chair and sat next to his dad. "So do we like him for you?"

Noah couldn't meet his son's frank gaze. "He's sort of on the… casual side."

Josh nodded. "Okay, so how do we fix him?"

"Josh, you can't just fix people! Not unless they want to change." Noah shook his head.

"Da-ad! You built a life for us from nothing. Raised me on your own. You don't think you're up to taking on the Chief?"

Noah's lips quirked. "I'm not sure I want to, Josh. Fix him… hmm."

Josh cocked a brow in satisfaction. He'd given his lonely dad a little push in the right direction.

JADE took a deep drag of her cigarette, eyes carefully on Kell, as if she wanted to ignore the waiting and ever-hopeful Alec, who had showed up to lean against the archway into her kitchen. "There, uh, might have been something moving through the woods. But it could have been a shadow...."

"Noah and Josh reported someone stole into their kitchen and helped themselves to some food around about the time you and Thomas were in the woods nearby," Kell said, scribbling on his pad. Thomas had mentioned it also.

"You mean it was the ghost? For real?" Jade asked.

Kell's mouth firmed at the word "ghost." "What happened then?"

"Thomas kind of freaked out since he was sure he saw someone moving through the forest, and I sneezed."

Kell blinked. "Sneezed."

"Yeah, it was damp out there, right?" She crinkled her forehead. "I don't like the woods much because the damp bothers my sinuses."

"And then?" Kell pressed, leaning forward.

"I yelled at Thomas after the gun went off and he shoved me—" Jade was breathing fast, remembering.

"*Goddamn that kid!*" Alec swore softly.

"Hey, he was scared and I was scared." She could admit it now after seeing Morley. "I hit something, like a tree? And then I guess I blacked out."

Kell nodded, reaching out to squeeze Jade's hand gently. "But we found you and you're safe."

"Chief, if the ghost is for real and it killed Morley...." Her voice drifted off. "I feel...."

"Like what, Jade?" Kell asked patiently.

"Like I miss my dog," Jade confessed softly.

Kell shifted in his chair, looking up to meet Alec's concerned gaze. "Jade, we're going to do our best to get to the bottom of this. Soon. You have my word."

"Yeah, guess when it was just going through people's garbage it wasn't a big priority," Jade noted. "But it's all over town it ate Morley."

Kell shook his head ruefully. In a small town, he'd known it would be all over in no time, along with the idea this was some kind of supernatural something prowling the mountain. There'd been rumors of that for years. "We don't know what all happened to him. But I don't want you worrying. You got off with a bad headache but you're going to be okay. Likely it's someone who had a grudge against Morley, possibly over his crop or his habit of spying on folks."

Jade sighed. "I hope you're right, Chief. Truth is, I always thought the ghost thing was bogus. Thought it was just someone hungry out there."

A FEW hours later, Kell popped some Advil with a shot of cold coffee. He'd been staring at the same witness reports from Jade and Thomas, as well as the initial report on Morley Orris. Alec had yet to find any solid leads on who might have killed Orris, but it was a small town, and that narrowed down the suspects, if Kell discounted the ghost theory.

"Hi," Noah said softly, interrupting with a knock on Kell's open office door.

Kell looked up from his notes and felt electricity move through his body, recharging him. *Noah!* Noah was here.

"Hi! Come on in and…. Here, I'll fix the chair." Kell shoved paperwork off the wooden seat that faced his desk. He scrubbed a hand through his hair, wishing he'd known Noah was coming, because his space wasn't neat the way Noah's was. Did that count in Noah's eyes? And why the hell was he so worried about that?

"I came by to ask for your help."

Kell immediately stiffened. "Josh's okay?"

Noah smiled, his gray eyes softening into a misty spring sky. "Yes, he is. He's at the library now. He did, uh, have a few questions about us."

"Us." Kell blinked, feeling a blush working up his neck. Shit! "You mean…?"

"Yeah."

"It's not easy, you being his father. Do you want me to speak to him?"

"No!" As if seeing the quick flash of rejection Kell experienced, Noah continued, "I think this is something we have to work out."

"Right." Kell sat on the edge of his desk, not wanting to crowd Noah since he'd come here, but needing to be close to him. Man, he had it bad! "So, uh, what can I do for you?"

"I wondered if you knew anything about this Sheltie rescue site? The breeder seeks homes for mature dogs and not just puppies."

"You're getting one?" Kell's eyes widened as he thought about the ramifications. It sounded like despite the problems haunting the area, Noah and Josh intended to stay.

"I thought Josh would want a puppy, but we talked about it and now we are both leaning toward providing a home for an older, unwanted Sheltie; that's a Shetland Sheepdog."

Kell nodded. "I know what it is. I guess getting a dog means you're here for a while, huh?" He flushed at Noah's look of amusement over his transparent fishing and cleared his throat. "Yes, I know this breeder. She works at the coffee shop part-time. I hear her dogs are well cared for, if you want a Sheltie and not just a mutt."

Noah gave Kell a meaningful look. "I like mutts too."

"Oh, do you?" Kell felt his body warm as Noah danced with him. "That's good. Uh… very good. Because I'm purebred mongrel."

"You certainly are." But Noah's tone was caressing as he held Kell's eyes. "Would she be at the coffee house this time of day?"

"Yep, I'll get you the address, but it's just down the street." Kell grabbed a pen, muttering to himself a little. He was acting like a complete dweeb and all because Noah had shown up at his office. He scribbled down the coffee shop location. "And the local vet is a nice lady. You might drop by and get her advice. Her office is next to the bakery."

Noah took the slip of paper, standing. He shrugged, looking as awkward as Kell felt now he'd got what he'd come for. "Thank you."

"Can I...? Uh, are you in town long enough to grab a meal with me at the diner? You and Josh, I mean?" Kell blurted.

Noah paused and then smiled, that smile going straight to Kell's balls and making them tighten deliciously. "Every stereotype I've ever heard about small towns is if you have a meal with someone in the diner, it's all over town they are a thing. Is that the case here?"

"Yep, I suppose it's a stereotype for a reason," Kell allowed wryly. Noah was still holding his eyes, seeming surer of himself than when Kell first hit on him. He liked unsettled Noah, but he *really* liked standing-on-his-own-feet Noah.

"And that's not a problem for you?" Noah was asking many questions with just the one.

Kell got the message. "Nope, not here."

"Yes, okay, we'd like to eat with you," Noah agreed, blushing.

Kell decided he liked blushing Noah best of all.

Chapter 8

"JADE, it's getting dark. We should head back," Alec suggested after hours of searching for Jade's dog in the woods near her home. Not that he wasn't enjoying spending time with her—any chance for that, except he didn't like seeing the dark circles under her eyes, the big lump on her forehead, or her skin pale under the light dusting of freckles he'd fantasized about kissing.

Jade kicked a nearby tree and then put her hands on her hips, huffing for breath since she'd been racing ahead of Alec on the deer trails. She obviously spent a lot of time hiking, because she was in great shape, something else to appreciate about her. Alec sighed. Was there anything about this unattainable woman that didn't appeal to him?

Reading the worry under the spark of frustration, Alec dared to cup the back of her neck, and when she swung around to glare at him, he pushed her hair out of her face. Her pupils were dark, swallowing his reflection; he felt like he could fall into her eyes.

"Yeah, well, if you're givin' up—"

"Not giving up. I don't give up anything I want so easy," Alec said, smiling slightly. Slow and steady, he reminded himself. He'd been trying to figure out what might work to bring her closer to him, and he'd figured that was the best strategy. "I know you're frantic but it's going to be dark soon. I'll be back first thing in the morning to help you look for Beau again, okay? But we could mess up any tracks out here or just get lost. It's time to give it a rest."

Jade nodded reluctantly. "But I *hate* waiting," she grouched as they headed downhill toward her house, windows streaming with a lemon beacon like a welcome lighthouse.

"I noticed, but some things are better if you have to wait for them." Alec cocked a brow.

"What, you one of those guys who brags about what a slow fuck you are?" She gave him a scathing glance. Alec knew she was covering her upset by scratching him, but he would wear her scratches if he had to. Hell, he *wanted* to.

Anything for Jade, whom he'd loved since he was fifteen years old and she was a wild, untamed beauty of twenty-two.

"Don't need to brag," he said, and he hid a smile when she glared at him. But he didn't miss the slow, considering look she gave him: he had her thinking about it, and that was good. He hadn't lied about waiting. He'd waited for years to be man enough she'd take him seriously. He'd still be waiting when he was sixty-eight and she was seventy-five, if that were how long it took.

"It gets dark here quick, huh?" Jade commented. "I never noticed before, but...." She bit her lip. "Shit, I wish we'd found my dog. The house does seem totally empty."

The deerskin bundle around Alec's neck began to warm faintly, and he grabbed it, tensing. *Something....*

"Yeah." He looked over his shoulder at tall stands of moss-covered trees, slick with the cool humidity that even the hottest summer days couldn't burn away.

Jade gave him a speculative look. "There's something you *know* about whatever haunts these woods, isn't there? Something you haven't told anyone."

Alec looked at Jade, crediting her with reading him better than almost anyone, except maybe Kell. "Maybe."

WYLDE watched the couple as they headed back down the trail that led to the woman's house. Sometimes when she baked cookies, she left them out on a plate, as if for the birds. He'd eaten them many times, closing his eyes and savoring the sweet, perfect taste.

The young man with the woman made Wylde feel funny, the way he did sometimes. He wondered if he'd have dreams about him, dreams of touching his skin.

"SO WHAT are your intentions toward my dad?" Josh demanded as soon as Kell put his hat down on the bench beside him in the diner and sat facing him and Noah.

Kell swallowed under the steady look from two pairs of gray eyes, wishing for whiskey and not coffee in that moment. Clearly, if he took on Noah, he was also taking on Josh.

Well, he was up to it.

"My... what?" Kell glanced at Noah in shock and saw color flush his cheeks. He wanted to lick him where the color lit his cheekbones, dig his fingers into Noah's love-sweaty hair as he moved inside him—

He dragged his eyes and his libido away from Noah and looked to Josh, who had a stack of books on their table from his visit to the library—Kell noticed that some were about Shetland Sheepdogs, and some about ghost hunters. Shit.

Josh calmly continued to regard Kell with his hands folded over his collection.

"Uh...."

"Dad tells me you don't take stuff too serious," Josh continued. "And I want to be straight with you... you're okay with that, right?" For a moment, vulnerability moved through Josh's gray eyes and reminded Kell he was very young.

"I prefer a straight shooter, yeah," Kell said, wondering what he was leaving himself open for. One thing was for sure; this kid was going to be a helluva man one day.

"We like you for my Dad, but you need some work."

Kell didn't know what to say. He glared at Noah, who was now stifling laughter.

"Is that right?"

"Yep. So I found some books for you at the library." Josh pushed a portion Kell had missed from the heavy pile toward him.

"Josh—"

"Do you want my Dad or not?" Josh flatly demanded.

Kell's gaze heated as he looked at Noah, watching the laughter die in those gray eyes and give way to that shy look. He liked to make Noah shy. He liked that Noah responded to him, whether it was anger, scratching, whateverthefuck! Kell would take him on, take it all on....

"I... yeah," Kell rasped, knowing his eyes must signal his intensity as they held Noah's. "I want your dad very, very much."

"Then you have to read up, Chief. Dad tells me education is everything. I did some reading too, about bi men, but I had to hit some websites for that."

Kell met Noah's gaze, seeing he was now chewing his lip. He figured Noah was probably not bi, but gay, but he probably didn't want to shake his son's belief in whatever his relationship had been with Josh's mother. He could respect that.

"Do you have any questions?"

"I have to get used to the water, I think," Josh reflected. "Like when the pool isn't what you expected."

"You mean when it's a delicate shade of purple?" Kell joked, teasing Josh gently about his pool. "Your Dad and I don't want to freak you out. I just want you to know that...." Kell thought there was one thing he could say to put Josh's mind at rest. "You come first with him and you should. You're lucky to have him, Josh, but maybe you'll let me… date him."

Josh let out a breath. "Okay, you're a bit rough around the edges, but maybe there's hope since you seem to want to change."

"Huh?" Kell glanced at the title of the topmost book: *Courting rituals of Victorian Times.* Holy shit! "Josh—"

"Don't worry, Chief. We'll make you into a good boyfriend for my Dad in no time. That is if you want to date us?"

Us? Kell's eyes widened as he confronted again that he was taking on more than Noah here. As much as he wanted to drag Noah to a nice warm cave somewhere and have his way with him, Noah was a single father, and Josh was part of the deal.

Kell put down his menu. "I haven't…." He cleared his throat. "I haven't dated anyone before, Josh. But, uh, I would be happy to try. That is if you can give me a hand?"

The satisfied smile on Josh's face squeezed Kell's heart even as he told himself it was no big deal. So he'd have to observe a few niceties before taking Noah to bed. It didn't mean he was getting in deep with him. It didn't mean they'd really be anything but a casual couple.

"YEAH, well, she's a lying bitch, what can I say?" Thomas Anderson told his friend over the phone. He was sprawled on the carpeted floor of the empty music room above his parents' triple garage. The architecture jutted out into the woods, but Thomas refused to be scared anymore about the shadow he sometimes thought he saw in the mist or the strange young man he'd glimpsed the night the Chief had rescued him. He had nightmares, sure, but everything was fading now, and mostly he was worried what his school friends would think if Jade Moreton spilled what had happened that night.

So he'd decided not to wait for her to make him look bad. He was going to beat her to it. No one would believe her if he trashed her first. And anyway, his mom had fired her, and everyone in this small town knew that too.

"Look, I don't care what rumors you heard from your buddy the deputy. I didn't run away. I... just got lost. Yeah, okay, see you at the game tomorrow."

Thomas put down the phone, biting his lip. It didn't sound like Marty had believed him. Well, fuck, Marty hadn't been there. Too bad all that pot was gone along with Morley, because Thomas could really use some now to mellow out.

He sighed. Maybe it was just as well. The one time Morley had come by the house, Thomas's dad had been home. He hadn't seemed to like what he saw of Morley and warned Thomas to stay away from him. Thomas's mom was cold and remote, but Thomas was used to that from her. The old man, though... Thomas did his best never to cross him. Especially lately, since he was in an unpredictable mood, thankfully spending a lot of time hunting and fishing in the forest.

From below, the garbage cans he'd left outside rattled. "Shit." Second time this week. If his mom fucking heard it—

"*Thomas!*" the intercom blared, his mom's icy disapproval entering the room like an unpleasant vapor. "You left those cans out again and someone's dog is in them!"

Thomas got up and pounded "answer." "Yeah, yeah, sorry, Mom. Forgot about 'em."

"See if you can find Minny while you're bringing them back into the garage. I think she's hiding again."

His mom's cat, a Persian named Minny, never left their house, so they'd had to set up a litter box for her in the garage. One of Thomas's sucky jobs was emptying it once a day into the trash now that his mom had fired Jade. He sighed. "Yeah, okay, Mom...."

JOSH was drawing as Noah and Kell finished off their burgers.

"Good?" Kell asked as he watched Noah lick his lips.

"Amazing! I'd never thought such simple food could taste so good, but I'll have to take up running again at this rate."

Kell cocked a brow. "You keep in nice shape. I'm sure you have a lot of stamina."

Noah blushed, no fool to the subtext. "Thanks. So I thought we'd find our Shetland Sheepdog tomorrow."

Kell nodded, eating a fry. He didn't want them to leave, even knowing that with Josh around, he couldn't exactly do the things with Noah he wanted. He just didn't want them to leave just yet. "How about a movie tonight?"

"Something cool?" Josh demanded, slapping his sketch down.

Noah met Kell's amused gaze. "Okay, but if you get frightened by the gore—" Noah began.

"*Da-ad!* Totally don't embarrass me, okay?"

Kell frowned, reaching for Josh's drawing when something struck him as familiar about it.

A pale face looking into a window. Lost, lonely eyes, long dark hair. Tall trees looming misty behind the figure. The face and tormented expression reminded him of his recent dream.

"Josh, is there something you want to talk about?" he asked.

Josh helped himself to his dad's fries, but his face was sober. "Not yet...."

THOMAS cursed when he tried the light switch in the garage and nothing happened. Why had his parents wanted to live in this fucking place? Oh, yeah, because when they had lived in L.A., they'd fought all the time, his father convinced his mom was screwing around on him. So the old man had moved them out here, to the wilderness. But the power was always going out, another sucky thing about living here. He opened the cabinet by the door between house and garage and located a flashlight, turning it on and shining it over the cavernous space, taking in his muddy Toyota, his mom's Lexus and his dad's BMW.

"Minny?" he called.

He heard another rattling sound. Sweat prickled the back of his neck.

"Stupid cat," he whispered. "Stupid fucking cat."

KELL paid for popcorn, drinks and candy for all three of them, feeling good about treating his two dates. Josh gave him brief thanks and snagged his share, racing for the theater where the movie was showing.

Kell grinned. "I think he's afraid you'll change your mind," he told Noah, referring to how they were seeing a more adult action-adventure film.

Noah shook his head. "He's not spoiled but... I probably let him do too many things."

"Nah, I disagree. I think you're doing a fine job."

"Yeah?" Noah gave him another shy smile, making Kell's balls tighten in response. He couldn't take it anymore. He needed to touch, taste, *claim* Noah.

"Betsy, will you hold onto our treats for just two seconds?" Kell abruptly asked.

The girl at the counter nodded, and Kell led Noah away from the movie crowd to a deserted alcove.

"Kell?" Noah's eyes were full of uncertainty, but he'd allowed himself to be cut from the crowd. That spoke volumes about his willingness to be wooed.

Once in the shadows, behind some tall potted plants, Kell carefully took Noah in his arms, dark eyes holding gray ones. Asking. Giving plenty of time. And then his mouth closed warmly over Noah's, hot and demanding, drinking him in with a long, drawn-out moan of relief. *Noah.*

Noah parted his lips, and Kell rewarded him with a slow, luscious tongue-fuck, lifting him high against the wall and placing his bigger body between Noah's legs. He let the hungry knob of his erection rub gently back and forth against Noah's smaller body until he felt Noah begin to grow hard.

"Put your legs around my hips." Kell growled out the order in a guttural tone.

Noah complied, his head falling back as Kell thrust against him, sprinkling scalding little kisses down his neck. Shit! He broke away, panting, huge and swollen and on the very edge of his control. Noah was gripping his forearms, eyes wide in his face.

"*Oh, Jesus!*" Kell rasped, leaning his forehead against Noah's. "You need to lay down for me. Please, baby, make it soon...."

RWRAWHHHHHRRRRRR!

"*Fucking cat!*" Thomas yanked his bleeding hand away, shaking it. Minny was high up on a cupboard, eyes huge and yellow in the darkness. She hissed indignantly, her small body pulled tight against the wall. "What's your problem? I'm just trying to bring you inside. Fuck it! Fine, just stay out here!"

The crash of metal came again from the specially reinforced bear-proof trashcans his parents used. Thomas stiffened, feeling a little freaked, though he knew it was just someone's dog or maybe a coyote. He'd certainly seen one of those around often enough. It couldn't be the ghost... Thomas was sure he'd seen fear in the young man's eyes, as if he didn't want to be seen.

Heart pounding in his throat, he headed for the door out of the garage to retrieve them. His mom would give him shit if he didn't, and he wanted her off his ass. Yet he came to a dead stop five feet from the door—the door that was hanging open, gently swaying back and forth in the night breeze off the mountain.

The door he hadn't opened....

He backed away one careful step at a time, barely breathing.

He only had to make it inside the house. Get to his Dad's guns. They'd call the Chief—

A soft scuffling sound. He wasn't alone in here.

He frantically bounced the flashlight around, hand trembling, glaring light catching emptily off the windows and headlights of silent vehicles.

The intercom suddenly blasted, scaring the shit out of him. "Thomas, did you take care of those garbage cans?"

Thomas charged for the door into the house, scrabbling for the latch. Enough was enough!

"*Mo*—*!*" Thomas huffed, in such a hurry to open the door that he dropped the flashlight. It bounced in a hard arc, lighting something red and liquid pooled in front of the cars.

Chapter 9

NOAH leaned against the wall, his legs trembling from the force of his awakening passion. He was hard and aching, and his body was singing under Kell's skillful and ardent touch. How could this be happening so fast? He hadn't even known this man a few days ago. Then he'd been annoyed by him, thought him a pushy hick.

Now part of him wanted to do what Kell wanted. Lie under him. And Kell was right, damn him, because part of Noah was a little gun shy, but for more reason than Kell had so far sensed, thank God.

"Kell, should we...? Anyone could see us here," Noah rasped, not sure he wanted to leave Kell's hands, his arms, except he was a responsible adult, and his son was in the darkened theater waiting for them. Shit!

Kell kissed his lips and then pressed more hot kisses against his neck. "I wish they could see you, see how I make you feel. If we lived a couple of thousand years ago, I'd parade you naked wearing my collar...."

Noah burst into shocked laughter and smacked Kell's shoulder. "You are *so* retro, Chief! But this is... too much, too soon. I've never felt this way."

As if seeing Noah was growing upset in the wake of their near-sex, Kell took a deep breath and pulled away, his head back, panting.

Noah stared, wide-eyed. Had he really had that kind of powerful effect on Kell, a seasoned lover? Noah had barely any experience with another man.

"Okay, you're not ready for the big gay make out in semi-public places," Kell breathed, muscled chest still heaving. His voice was raspy, sexy to Noah's ears. "But you'll star tonight in my very own private movie as my submissive and...." Kell swallowed, reaching out to stroke Noah's hair. His hand wasn't quite steady, Noah noticed, hyper-aware of everything about this man. "Beautiful Noah-slave. That all right by you? A fella can dream."

Noah flushed but then nodded. "Thank you for understanding."

"How about the big gay make out in private places?" Kell pushed, dark eyes twinkling. "You ready for that?"

Noah laughed and shoved Kell away. "I think we both better stay in this alcove until what we are feeling isn't too... obvious."

Kell stepped back. "If I stay here, I'm going to touch you and you're going to like it. And I won't be able to stop myself from making you come, Noah. So I'm going to gather our popcorn and drinks and go find Josh. See you in a few."

Noah watched the larger man stride away and thought it was very Kell that he obviously didn't care his erection was tenting his jeans. The Chief was a true alpha male.

Noah knew it wasn't PC to like the way such a man treated him, but... it seemed he had a weakness for bossy, take-charge alpha males. He rubbed his damp forehead ruefully. By rights, Kell was treading on unhealed ground, so why wasn't he setting off Noah's trip wires? But the truth was, from the beginning, Noah had felt completely safe with Kell. The Chief liked to kiss, tease, *lure* him into play, but he listened to Noah, respected Noah's limits.

Noah huffed out a breath. Kell was an irresistible combination, and he knew it, damn him.

"THIS is so great!" Josh crowed when Noah had calmed enough to rejoin him and Kell. Noah felt his heart melt a little when he saw Kell was sitting on one side of Josh so that Noah could sit on the other, because some of Noah's previous dates would have insisted on sitting next to him, maybe wanting to make out with Noah during the movie, ignoring Josh.

Not that Noah would let them forget his son!

But his barbarian truly seemed to care about Josh.

Irresistible.

KELL'S cell phone vibrated, and he immediately tensed, placing it by his ear while he glanced at Noah. In another moment, he snapped it closed and reached across Josh to lightly squeeze Noah's shoulder, silently telling him he had to leave.

Noah's gaze followed him as he left the theater, but he could already see that Kell was a million miles away, his mind on his job. For some reason, his heartbeat picked up, and unease pricked him, but he shoved it aside, putting an arm around Josh and trying to lose himself in his son's innocent enthusiasm for the movie.

He guessed this was part of dating a lawman, if that was what he was doing.

"VICTIM identified as… a raccoon, found by Thomas Anderson." Daniel Makepeace looked over at Kell. "And I remind you, Chief, I am not qualified to deal with small wild animals. But because you called me in anyway, I can tell you that the cause of death appears to be… massive tissue loss." Daniel Makepeace spoke into his recorder, voice sober, since he was shaken, as they all were, by another mysterious and frightening event in their town. He stood up for a moment, pausing, head down before shaking his head and then continuing.

Kell and deputy-on-loan Alec Danvers waited just beyond the garage, watching the coroner as he examined the scene. "I appreciate you lookin' anyway, Daniel," Kell said. "It will help with my investigation."

"Hmm." Makepeace snapped his measuring tape closed. "Height and weight of raccoon can only be estimated at this time...."

Kell turned away, closing his eyes and breathing deeply. There was bloody raccoon spread all over this garage, but Kell's personal nightmare was that it could just have easily have been seventeen-year-old boy. And the Andersons didn't live too far away from Noah and Josh.

"The torso has been severed, skin peeled back. All the major organs are missing." Daniel's eyes caught Kell's, reminding him of how they'd found Morley in much the same state. Kell's lips tightened since they'd only just begun digging into Morley's life, looking for his killer, and now this had happened.

He stared at the word scrawled in scarlet across the paved garage floor. *Don't.* Clearly it was some kind of message to someone... like Morley had been? What had Alec called his body, a scarecrow?

Alec had knelt by the door into the garage, carefully examining it. "Some deep scratch marks here, Chief, but they are inconclusive; could have been here quite some time."

Kell bent close to his deputy, taking in the scoring marks. Then he remembered something. "Why do I get a feeling that someone is being sent a message?"

"I have the same feeling," Alec noted. "Territory."

"It could be the homeless 'ghost' doing this, only... Alec, the reason no one in this town ever got too worked up was he or she never hurt anyone before. Now…" Kell muttered. Then he rubbed his jaw. "Shit."

Alec only looked at him, mute. Kell knew he had some ideas, but it was typical of his deputy to sit on them until he was ready to share.

Inside the garage, Makepeace continued to document his findings. He pulled something from underneath the muddy Toyota, and Kell swallowed, feeling sick, even though it was just an animal. Shit! "Detached left limb, severed with what looks like a handmade blade…."

"DANIEL…." Kell leaned opposite Makepeace against the coroner's SUV. The other man was unsnapping his plastic gloves in jerky movements.

"I don't know!" For once, laconic Daniel looked almost weary. The shock of the scare to a teenage boy in their small, out-of-the-way little town had hit even him. It was that way for all of them, law enforcement and hospital staff, when they dealt with kids.

"I need something to go on. I have to solve this case fast, before folks start shooting at shadows and maybe hurt someone."

Makepeace shook his head. "I think it's the same knife used on Morley, but that's all I can tell you."

"Why? What does 'don't' mean?" Kell prodded aloud, feeling helpless. One person was dead and now this, soon after. Something was stirred up, and he had to get to the bottom of it soon.

So he could hunt this killer.

The two men stared at each other.

Kell growled softly. "The whole town seems to believe in this nonsense about some kind of ghost being responsible, but we have to keep our heads or we'll never find who is responsible."

"I can only tell you my findings based on the physical evidence presented from Morley Orris and the raccoon's remains. If this is a deranged hunter doing this… frankly, he's giving me the creeps!"

"Okay, Daniel." Kell looked reluctantly toward the house, the living room lit as the shocked parents were comforted by neighbors. He stared at Mylar Anderson, his hand clenched on his wife Marisa's shoulder. The man really seemed attached to her, despite how cold she was and the fact that Kell himself had caught her being unfaithful. Probably it wasn't the first time. Had the word "don't" referred to her somehow?

"I can tell you it's a very efficient killer. And I don't think it's going to stop."

"Why do you say that?"

"I don't know, except… so far it's winning."

Kell glared at the dark forest. "So I'll make it stop."

KELL took a deep breath two hours later as he sat in his SUV. He needed to head inside, talk to Noah, but he had to ground himself first. He got out of the vehicle and rubbed his aching temples, his gaze catching on Josh, who was watching him with a sober expression from his bedroom window.

He had managed to get Thomas to confess to buying pot from Morley Orris. Thomas also remembered inviting Orris to his home a few times.

The connecting thread Kell had been looking for—Thomas had known Orris, done business with him—led him… where?

In another moment, he was striding for the front door.

"How was the movie?" Kell asked Noah when the other man opened his door.

"I'm not sure Josh will sleep he was so excited; he loves science fiction." Noah smiled. Then he seemed to absorb the weariness and tension coming from Kell.

"Something's wrong." He reached out, his hand almost making contact with Kell's arm before he let it fall.

"Thomas Anderson; he had a real scare," Kell stated flatly.

"Another one? He didn't get lost again, did he?" Noah walked into his living room, studying Kell sharply.

"Noah, you live even further up the mountain than the Andersons do. I'm worried about you and Josh," Kell said as he followed Noah into the living room. "I don't know what the hell is going on right now, but no, he didn't get lost this time."

"My God! That poor kid and his parents!" Noah shook his head, obviously in shock. "Kell, what happened, can you talk about it?"

"Thomas found a dead raccoon in his garage. It looks like someone left it there deliberately. Listen, I want you and Josh to move in with me just until I stop this from happening."

Noah's eyes widened. "We barely know you!"

"Or let me stay here with you at night," Kell pleaded, his fists balled. "I won't make a play for you if you aren't ready, but I just need to keep you both safe. Please, Noah."

PLEASE. Not a word he thought came easily from Kell, but one he used because he cared what happened to Noah, to Josh.

"Kell." Noah could feel waves of determination coming from his Chief. He had the sense that this man would die before he let anything happen to him and his son. It made him even more attracted to the man, as he had been in the theater when Kell had put Josh first, even before seducing Noah.

"He was just a kid," Kell muttered, looking away. "And somehow I fucked up, missed something, and he got scared. In my town, Noah."

"Kell, don't do this." Noah took his arm, finding the muscles rigid. It was gut-wrenching, envisioning how he'd feel as a parent if Josh were hurt. Kell seemed to take on the role of guardian of the whole town. "You saved his life just recently, remember? Come on, I have some tofu brownies and hot joe in the kitchen."

Kell blinked. "You gotta be fucking kidding. You put *tofu* in brownies? You really are from Seattle."

Glad to distract Kell, Noah nodded, smiling a little, leading the larger man into the large, warm space where copper pots hung and herbs bloomed in the window over the sink. Beyond the windows, the landscaping lit the night. For some reason, Noah now left those lights on during the hours of darkness, as if the illumination pushed back the woods beyond.

"It keeps them moist. They're good, trust me."

He poured Kell a cup of coffee, not asking if he wanted decaf, since he had an idea that he'd get an emphatic rejection to that suggestion. Then while Kell watched, he sliced a fresh brownie slathered with thick glossy icing.

He passed both to Kell and sat down, sipping from his own cup.

Kell picked up the brownie and looked at it suspiciously. "You baked it yourself?" he asked.

"Yep. Try it. I haven't killed anyone yet with my cooking."

Kell took a bite, and the tired lines on his face relaxed a little. "Huh."

Noah's lips pressed together, suppressing a smile; Kell liked the brownie. But he wasn't prepared for his Chief to lean forward and touch his arm. "Please let me take care of you, baby. It would kill me if anything happened to you or Josh."

Chapter 10

"A MISSING person in our town, yes. And I think it has to go back some time, Daniel," Kell spoke softly into the phone in Noah's home office, gazing out at the woods as the sun flamed yellow and orange through the top branches. It was beautiful here, but his neck was stiff from lack of sleep and the tension of staying up all night.

He'd rested with his gun lying on the bedside table of Noah's guest room.

Noah had been stubborn about coming down from Sullivan's Mountain to stay with him. He had all kinds of excuses, and Kell guessed they were good ones; after all, the other man barely knew Kell, and Kell's house was not as large as Noah's. It didn't even have an extra bedroom where Noah and Josh might stay, but he broke out in a cold sweat when he thought of them all alone up here. So he was staying, even if he had to sleep out in his truck to watch over them. Fortunately, that hadn't been necessary, as Noah had offered him the use of his guest room again.

Now Noah walked in wearing a robe, his hair in soft curls around his face, sipping some hot, dark Seattle coffee. Kell immediately felt the familiar stirring of his sex, as if he were an animal catching the scent of his mate.

Noah handed him some coffee, the crisp roast of high-end beans rising between them like the finest incense. Kell sipped, feeling ridiculously like he was caught in a romantic coffee ad, but it didn't stop him from reaching out to smooth a reverent hand through Noah's silky hair. He stopped short of closing his eyes and pressing against Noah to breathe in his scent only because he was still on the phone.

Simmering, he watched as Noah flicked him a shy glance before giving a tactful nod, leaving Kell to finish his call. The blond picked up a fluffy jumbo towel and retreated out the French doors for a morning swim.

Kell watched him with narrowed eyes as he listened to Daniel continue, "You asked Alec and I to dig into the town's past and see if any of the citizens ever just up and... disappeared. Well, turns out you might have something, Kell."

"Hmm, that would be good, since so far I feel like we're in the dark. We need some facts, not vague stories," Kell said, frowning. "So what did you and Alec find out, going through the town records?"

Do you think we're safe here? Noah had asked him. Maybe not, but Kell was going to do something about that, by damn.

"Well, the old man who lived in Noah's house, Mr. Butler, was an avid gardener. I'm sure you've seen remains of his work since it's rumored your truck is up there...." Daniel coughed but Kell said nothing. He'd figured that people would start to talk about him and Noah soon enough. "He was a bit of an eccentric, judging by the purple pool. And for one year before he was discovered dead in that house, he had a grandson registered for homeschooling. There is no record of him after Butler's death." Kell heard the creak of a chair over the phone and pictured Daniel leaning back, no doubt as tired as Kell was. "So there may have been a seven-year-old boy up there at one time and I can't find any trace of him showing up in the system for the State of Washington after the homeschooling records ceased."

"What the hell? How could that happen?" Kell demanded. Seven years old?

"I don't know, Kell. It's very strange. But you know Sullivan's Mountain has a lot of unexplored forest, including lots of box canyons. It's easy to get lost up there."

"But not easy to survive. A child... how would he even find food?" Kell blinked. "You think this might be our ghost?"

"That's your job, Chief," Daniel said. "It's as likely the boy didn't survive, or he might have run away or some other relatives came and claimed him."

"Uh huh." Kell found it hard to believe folks in town hadn't had any contact with this boy, especially since years ago, it would have been an even more intimate place. "Who might have met the child around the time he would have been here to take that home schooling?" Kell asked.

"I think our librarian had just started around then," Daniel mused. "I'm not sure if any of the teachers at the school would have, since the boy was being home schooled. In fact, it seems like old man Butler went to a lot of trouble to keep the kid at home. Even back then you had to do a lot of paperwork to go that education route."

"Hmm. Well, everyone who knew the old man says he was an eccentric. Anyway, that's one old mystery," Kell noted in a tired voice. "The bigger one is who killed Morley and left that strange message in the Anderson's garage."

"No luck getting Noah and his son to come into town, huh?"

Shit. There were no secrets in this town. Had he been that obvious? He guessed so, but for some reason, his orientation had never bothered people here much. Maybe because Kell had always been matter-of-fact about it. Discreet when he had to be, like when he was in the army, but otherwise, he felt it was his business, and his business alone. Plus, folks liked how he did things, capable but not on everyone's ass. He let the townsfolk keep their secrets, and they tolerated his.

"No, not yet. You can reach me here if I'm not in the office or in the diner."

Daniel's voice smiled. "I met Josh in the library the other day. Smart kid. Interesting collection of books he was taking out."

Remembering the Victorian courting book by his bedside, Kell flushed. Damn, his wooing Noah really was all over town! He hoped Noah remained oblivious, or it might make him even more gun-shy. He muttered, "Yep. Get back to me soon if you learn anything more. And by the way, what was the kid's name?" Kell asked.

Daniel told him.

"JUST where do you think you're going?" Alec said that morning as he caught Jade before she could enter the woods on the rise above her house. He'd been heading up the mountain to confer with the Chief but on a hunch had stopped by Jade's to make sure she wasn't getting into trouble. Well, that and drop off what she was missing— company.

"What are you, my stalker now?" She glared at him, and he sighed. He'd thought they'd reached a point of almost-friendliness, but with Jade, it was always one step forward and two steps back. And he was tired. Tired and worried. When he looked at her dark, wild hair and red lips, her beauty was sometimes overlaid with pictures of finding her body in bloody chunks in the forest. It made him sick, those flashes. Were his visions real, or was he just living the same fears he knew were riding his friend Kell about his new love interest? Hell, Alec hadn't been surprised when the Chief told him he'd be camping out at the Matthews's house. He was thinking of doing that for Jade and risking her wrath.

Throat tight, he studied her, taking in her smooth, glowing skin, her lean body, ripe and female but unharmed. She was okay, and he was going to make sure she stayed that way, no matter what. He could understand how Kell felt about Noah, the need to protect. "If I have to be. Come on." He took her arm.

His touch seemed to set her off, so she tried to swat him, but her narrowed eyes signaled her intent; he knew her too well. He swung her into his arms with a laugh.

"You're in-fucking-sane, Danvers!" she huffed.

"I want you to meet my grandma," he said, liking the feel of her in his arms.

"I've met her, you dork, remember? It's a small town."

"But now I'm courting you for real, and besides, she offered to come by and visit with you today. Company, right?"

She gaped at him. "I'm not a personal charity project. Put me down!"

"Jade."

"It's embarrassing to be hauled around by you in front of your grandma," Jade hissed.

"Oh." Alec placed her on her feet, watching her stalk toward her porch, ignoring him. He guessed he'd pissed her off. The thought somehow didn't depress him the way it did when she just ignored him. He hid a grin and followed.

His grandma Ruth was smoothing wrinkled hands over her jeans, enjoying the sunshine on Jade's porch. She was wearing some silver earrings with a killer whale inscribed and a long necklace made of Peruvian pink opal nuggets Alec had purchased for her on a trip to South America while he was still in the army. He had bought an identical strand for Jade, but it was resting in a bedroom drawer in his house.

RUTH wore her long hair in a French braid, dark eyes outlined with blue eye shadow the same shade as her T-shirt and jeans. Those eyes fixed on Jade, seeming to strip away her layers and *see* her.

She was used to that look from Alec's Grandma Ruth, who had taught math to most of the kids in the local high school before she retired. She reached out and took the older woman's hand. "Your grandson? Is acting like a macho jerk."

Ruth nodded. "He has a thing for you; everyone knows. And he knows no man stands a chance with you unless he stands up."

"Hey, I'm not sure he stands any kind of 'chance', okay? I live alone because I like it and I'm doing fine on my own."

"Yep, I get that. But Alec asked me up here to help him find your dog," Ruth said. "Will you let me help you? You never were one to lean on folks, even when a smart woman would accept a little help."

Jade blinked, leaning against one wooden pillar on her porch. She wasn't sure what the old woman meant, except it was rumored she had supernatural gifts. "Right. Well, I think the best way to find Beau is to head up the mountain and call his name," Jade said. "Which was what I was doing when your grandson interrupted me. Beau has disappeared sometimes in the past for a few days, but I guess I'm just spooked and a bit worried about him right now." She cocked a derisive brow at Alec, but he'd settled against the other porch pillar, seemingly content to watch and listen to Jade's conversation with his grandmother.

"You can't shake Alec off your trail. As for the ghost in the woods, you did him a kindness once, and time will come when you'll be tested again."

Jade felt unsettled at the certainty in the woman's voice. She remembered now that Alec had some native blood, and his grandmother was half Haida, some kind of medicine woman.

"A kindness? I have no idea what you mean. But this is my place," Jade said flatly. "I'm staying."

Alec sighed and rubbed his neck, his hand going to the leather bundle he wore over his uniform. Jade took a minute to admit he looked mighty fine. Tall, dark, a muscled chest that was hinted through his clothing, and the shine of his eyes on her was soft.

"Didn't sleep well, worrying about the ghost?" Jade poked him.

"Jade, you haven't been to town yet so you probably don't know, but…." Now Alec looked really unhappy. "I came out here to check on you because a strange message was found in the Anderson's garage just after dusk last evening."

Jade swallowed thickly. "Shit, after that kid got lost in the woods they had more trouble?" Jade didn't like Marisa Anderson much, and Thomas had acted like a bit of a twit, but damn.

Alec's lips tightened. "Yeah, a word written in blood."

KELL took a minute to finish his coffee, drifting through Noah's new office, one of the rooms that had been furnished; Noah had told him they were leaving some empty to have renovated as soon as possible. Kell admitted to himself he was curious about the man he was so inexplicably drawn to. He guessed it was a combination of old-fashioned lust, wanting to be inside Noah, wanting to ride him, and the protectiveness brought on from his job.

They'd met under extraordinary circumstances, Kell hunting for a lost kid the night Noah had moved in. From his experiences in his Ranger days, he knew that those heightened feelings had probably intensified his attraction to Noah. It was raw, hot, primal. He wanted to tangle his fingers in Noah's hair, hear him cry out as he surrendered to Kell.

There were pictures on the bookcases, mainly of Josh at different ages, judging by his missing baby teeth in some of them. He beamed out from the photographs, the lighthouse at the center of Noah's life. There was one older photograph of a lovely woman with dark hair and a face shaped vaguely the same as Josh's. His mother? Kell realized he didn't know the story there, and he wanted to.

He wanted to know everything about Noah.

When he put his coffee cup down on Noah's desk in preparation for going outside and talking to him, a letter to Noah fluttered to the floor. Kell bent to pick it up and replace it.

He didn't mean to look, but something caught his eye.

Chapter 11

KELL was waiting when Noah finished his laps. He held out the Egyptian cotton terry robe for him, trying to shove down his feelings. Shit! "We need to talk," he stated grimly.

"If this is about me moving in with you again," Noah began, looking pissy, "I've already given you my reasons and Josh and I are agreed we want some time in our new home, especially since someone is due here soon to do something about the, uh, purple pool."

"No, this is about your stalker! How long did you think you'd keep that a secret? Jesus, Noah! Now do you want to talk about it in the house where Josh might overhear, or out here?" Kell hated to push, but this was too important. Hell, he might have completely fucked up his approach to Noah and never known why.

"I—what? You're crazy!" But Noah was avoiding his gaze, his shoulders hunched as he pulled the towel tightly around himself like a protective cloak.

Kell felt his chest tighten. Someone had frightened Noah. He hadn't seen it at first, just taken his reserve for shyness, but when he'd come onto him at the theater, he'd sensed a trace of fear vibrating through Noah like a dark note on a tuning fork. He'd taken it for Noah's inexperience, and he'd gotten hot fast enough, so Kell hadn't thought twice about it.

"No, I'm not, baby," Kell said in a low tone, pulling Noah close and seeing heat sizzling in his gray eyes as well as the shadows. "Tell me. I need to know. I want to be your"—he sucked in a deep breath and then said it—"your lover. So I need to know. Do you think I'd ever want to do anything to scare you or turn you off? Jesus Christ!"

"I can't. I know it's irresponsible of me, but I can't talk about it, Kell. Especially not with you!" Noah squeezed his eyes shut. "One of the reasons I like being with you so much is you don't remind me of *him*."

When Kell touched Noah's shoulder, he could feel his skin felt chilly, and not just from the cool dip he'd taken. Shock.

"Why not me?" He forced himself to be gentle.

"Because I'm embarrassed. Because you are so forceful and confident and I want to hold my own with you and never have you consider me… less."

"That's not possible."

"Kell."

"Noah, I…." Kell stumbled again but made himself go even further out on a limb. "I like you."

"I like you too." There was a shy happiness in those shadows now, like a ray of light through thick trees.

Kell led Noah over to the private changing room behind the fountain, knowing Noah didn't want Josh exposed to whatever it was he was hiding. He pushed him onto a lounge chair and sat opposite him, reaching out to touch his face.

Noah flinched from his hand. The first time he'd ever done that. Shit!

Kell's mouth flattened as he leveled stern eyes on Noah. "Tell me who the son of a bitch was, Noah, so I can fucking rip out his guts!"

NOAH took a deep breath, shocked to find himself smiling when Kell growled out his orders like a grumpy bear. He looked like one too: unshaven, rumpled, with worry in his brown eyes as well as a clean kind of stubbornness. His large hand had fallen to his knee, the fingers well-shaped but battered, as if he did some carpentry. Noah could imagine him doing that, taking the time and patience to build something. No matter how hot for him Kell seemed to be, he was waiting on Noah.

"His name was Adam," Noah confessed in a voice just above a whisper. "He was a security consultant my condo building hired just after my wife's death. I'd always been attracted to men, and after she died I was so lonely, I thought it didn't matter anymore what I did, who I… associated with."

"He frightened you."

"Yes."

"Fuck!"

Suddenly Noah frowned. "Wait, how did you know about this? I'm sure I didn't give myself away, did I?"

Now Kell looked uncomfortable. "A letter from a private investigator you hired in Seattle to keep track of him. I didn't mean to read it but—"

Noah's eyes narrowed. "How dare you!"

Kell said flatly, "I'm not sorry."

KELL wasn't sure he could listen. He'd listened to other victims before, and it always made him sick, but this was Noah, his Noah. He forced himself to sit and wait. He'd opened this wound, and he had to be man enough for Noah to be there for him, no matter how it made him want to break rock with his bare hands.

"He was charming. Witty. Polished," Noah went on, and Kell felt a spark of jealousy. Sounded like this Adam had been everything Kell *wasn't*. Probably the fucker had approved of tofu too. "We attended functions together. Josh didn't know I was considering taking Adam as a lover, of course, since he was so young, still grieving for his mother. I made Adam wait for months before I would consider...."

"What happened?"

"One night I invited him up to our condo. I was considering ending the friendship. He'd grown impatient with what he referred to as my teasing him but increasingly I'd begun to find his intensity a little disconcerting. At first, I was flattered when he called me all the time, wanted to spend as much time as possible with me but... that night he pushed himself against me and I could feel he was hard. He touched my throat and suddenly my heart was... galloping. How could I have made such a mistake, read him wrong?" Noah's breath was hitching. "I just knew if I saw him again, he'd hurt me and maybe Josh."

Kell took Noah's cold hands in his own, holding onto him. "Noah, you couldn't know he was a fucking sleaze ball."

Noah looked at him and Kell hoped he could feel how Kell stood by him. "I didn't want Josh to know about Adam. I cut him from my life."

"You were protecting him! What if the asshole had really gotten rough? You didn't know." Kell rubbed Noah's back.

"It wasn't so bad. He never really did anything to me, but sometimes I'd see him in town and his eyes...."

Kell stroked Noah's hair. He said in what he thought was a reasonable voice, "I want to kill him. Tell me where he lives."

Noah choked out a wet laugh, burrowing closer as if he felt safe with hard, warm arms around him. Leaning as he probably rarely let himself lean since he was a single parent. "You can't protect Josh and me from the ghost if you're in jail, Chief," he scolded wryly.

"You'll let me stay?" Kell asked. "I haven't done anything to bring it back?"

"No." Noah's face glowed briefly. "You never bring it back. You can stay, Kell."

"SO YOU got some insight into what's doing all the bad mojo around here?" Jade asked Ruth, bringing her a glass of iced tea. She also gave one to Alec, which he took with an amused quirk of one dark brow, as if he'd known she'd been tempted not to offer him anything.

"Things are out of balance," Ruth mused, sipping the tea calmly. "They have been for a long time, since that boy went running off into the forest. Maybe I should have done something back then... maybe the whole town should have. We've all had plenty of opportunities, but now he is... hunted."

"Out of balance?" Jade wasn't sure exactly what the old woman meant, but it was true that things had felt off, though she had no idea who the old woman meant by the boy, unless it was... the ghost? Jade chewed her lip, remembering the cookies she habitually left outside. Was that the act of kindness the old woman had referred to?

The woman looked at Alec and pressed her lips together, as if she wanted to say more but thought better of it. She sighed and pulled a small pouch out from her pocket. "Stuff in there to help you find your lost dog, even though he's not really lost... but wait until Alec can go with you. There is something you two must do together. You are the ones who will help restore balance to our town."

"I NEED you to trust me to do something for you," Kell said. Noah was in his arms, and he kissed his damp curls, feeling that burning

104

need to take and own but harnessing it because now he understood the ugly black roots of Noah's fears.

"What?"

Kell stood and pulled Noah to his feet along with him, turning him around to face the change room floor-to-ceiling mirror. He slowly pulled the robe off Noah's slim, muscled shoulders so it puddled at his feet, leaving the other man in his damp swim trunks.

Kell clasped him warmly from behind, feeling the lean body tense and then relax when Kell didn't push. He kissed the side of Noah's neck and watched Noah follow the movement in the mirror.

"Baby, I want to give you a good time. I want to make you come and I want you to see me do it." Kell's big hand ran gently over the vulnerable crease between Noah's sex and his thigh.

"*Kell!*" Noah's face flushed as wide gray eyes held Kell's dark ones.

"Don't worry. I locked the change room door." Kell waited, rubbing patiently until he felt Noah's sex stiffen and grow from the tender almost-touching. "That's it, baby, so fucking beautiful." He kissed Noah's cheek, cradling Noah's body but making no effort to conceal his own aching erection, which he knew Noah must feel prodding him from behind. "Let me touch you now. Make you feel so good."

Noah's head fell back in surrender, and Kell tugged down his swimming trunks, freeing the pale, thick erection, which spilled into Kell's eager fist. "Look at that! Nice and long. Elegant like a fine racehorse," Kell praised.

"Are you saying I'm hung like a horse?" Noah tried to make a joke, but his voice cracked.

Kell could see this was hard for him, but he wanted to awaken Noah to how it should really be between two men, two lovers.

"The kind that's way too good for a rough mustang like me, yeah," Kell admitted ruefully. He snagged some baby oil that was handily available on the shelf with his free hand and squirted it generously onto his palm before working the warmed emollient over Noah's balls, squeezing them appreciatively. "Jesus, look at you. So smooth, baby. I like how you're shaved down there." His slick hand moved over the shaft, and Noah shuddered, his nipples hard pointing stars as Kell worked him.

"*OH MY God.*" Noah couldn't keep from thrusting. This! This is what he'd ached to feel for so long. Kell made him so hot, so fast, reducing Noah from his civilized self into a sensual, wanton creature, watching Kell's hands on him, taking control, but in an easy way, in a way that never made Noah feel afraid.

"Do you want me to get you off?" Kell purred in Noah's ear.

Noah shivered as Kell nipped his earlobe, his hand continuing to pump Noah as they both watched, his prick in Kell's possession.

"What the hell kind of question is that?" Noah growled, already on the verge and cranky at the idea of stopping. The oil magnified every sensation, so it felt like a velvet glove moving over him, taking him over.

Noah's arms slid up and back, winding around Kell's neck as he held his reflected gaze with heavy-lidded eyes before he studied himself, this slutty stranger, his lips flushed and his cheeks stung with color, panting helplessly as Kell jerked him, whimpering at the feel of Kell's experienced touch.

"Come on, baby, cream for me. You're so fucking gorgeous. You want to be my good boy, don't you? Come for me, I want to own you, want to know that only I can make you cream," Kell whispered directly into Noah's ear.

Noah shot, his come spilling lustily over Kell's fist as the big man continued to work him, making him whimper as he creamed again... and again....

Finally his body sagged trustingly against Kell's, and Noah huffed, completely satisfied.

"It's okay, baby. I got you. Knew you'd come like that. Just for me, your master, your lover, baby. So fucking beautiful," Kell praised, and Noah ate it up, hungry for praise. Hungry to feel a man.

Noah's wide eyes watched in the mirror as Kell put his hand to his lips and licked the taste of Noah from his fingers. "In my whole life, you're the most gorgeous thing I ever saw," Kell breathed.

Chapter 12

NOAH shoved his phone into the leather knapsack he'd brought with him into town so it rested like an unpleasant reminder amid the wild blackberries, goat's cheese, and Seattle-imported coffee he'd purchased. He'd even bought free-range eggs, since the next time he made Kell breakfast, he'd been willing to prepare something other than tofu for him.

The snake.

"Dad?"

He flinched and then took a deep breath, seeing from Josh's wide eyes that he'd worried him.

"Who was that on the phone?"

"No one." Oh, God. His son was so perceptive, and Noah never wanted him to know about this. "Do you want me to drop you off at the library?"

"Yeah, I should make sure the Chief returned my books." Josh's eyes twinkled. "From the way you guys were acting, I figured he'd done *some* reading."

Noah flushed, remembering Kell making him watch himself in the mirror. The rise of desire, the release. He'd felt a bit like a barbaric slave, performing for his master. So why had it turned him on so much? His mouth flattened, thinking of Kell now. "I have to see him."

"Uh oh. What did he do now?" Josh's eyes were a little cloudy with tension, reminding Noah that his son was new to his Dad dating at all, never mind another man.

"Nothing." Noah opened the door to their Toyota Tundra. "I'll come back to pick you up shortly."

"After you and the Chief fight."

"We are not going to—" Noah took a deep breath. "He trespassed, Josh."

"Yeah, I figured." Josh shrugged, looking out the window at the passing shops in town as they drove deeper into the village. "I know you are pretty uptight about having your own space, but I have a feeling he'll be doing that a lot."

Noah grunted, hands tightening on the wheel. He couldn't easily tolerate someone doing something without consulting him again. Not after Adam.

Josh glanced at him. "He really cares about you, more than I think even he knows. And when you care about someone, you screw up."

"THANKS for coming to see me, Mr. Anderson," Kell said, nodding as his visitor walked into his office. The business magnate nodded back, his face browned from a harsher sun than one that burned in the Pacific Northwest. Apparently he'd been in Australia for a while. His weathered hand gripped Kell's firmly, slate gray eyes assessing the lawman much as the Chief imagined they did the high-powered clients he handled.

"I came as soon as I could spare some time," Anderson said, settling in the chair Kell offered him. He folded his hands, looking completely unruffled, unlike most people, who usually had a residue of uneasiness visiting a lawman.

Kell frowned and leaned back in his own seat, tipping it as he studied the other man. "I'm sorry I have so far found no sign of the gun your son fired and lost in the woods."

The businessman cleared his throat, his pale eyes holding Kell's. He didn't have the stoop-shouldered physique Kell pictured for someone who spent long hours in an office, but he seemed a more active type, despite being well into his sixties. "That is a shame as it was a collector's item. I had forbidden Thomas to ever touch my gun cases and didn't even know he knew where the key to the locks were." The man's lips tightened. "And for the record, he's not really my son."

Kell blinked. He'd found if he went fishing, sometimes he turned up something unexpected. And so far all he knew was there were some strange goings-on up on Sullivan's Mountain, so talking to the few residents might shed some light. "Oh?"

"My wife and I got together shortly after he was born." Anderson smiled thinly before he took off his glasses and used a handkerchief to wipe them, looking thoughtful. "I married her and adopted Thomas because it was her wish and we have an... agreement."

"Uh huh." Kell's eyes narrowed, instinct kicking in. "Your son mentioned Morley Orris came to the house but you didn't seem to like him much?"

Anderson's face tightened. "I had a distaste for him. Thomas might have thought I was unaware of that man's side business, but there is little that goes on I miss."

"Well, certainly you'll agree that something strange is happening and people are getting hurt. I'm sure you want to help out with that, since your adopted son nearly got lost, and then someone broke into your garage and left that cryptic message."

"I have no idea why someone would threaten anyone in my family."

"Threat. Interesting that you take the word 'don't' to be a threat," Kell noted.

Anderson shrugged. "I'm sure I have no idea what it meant."

"Well, I have a theory that it could be a very personal message. Have you ever seen anything strange in the area?"

Anderson's eyes were opaque. "If you are speaking of the so-called ghost, then no, not personally."

"Your wife or son?"

"My wife thought there might be a homeless person in the area, yes. I ordered her to stop leaving food if that was the case," the businessman said primly. "There are, after all, places for such people."

"'Are there no work houses, are there no prisons...?'" Kell quoted Dickens softly, grimacing. "So you're saying you suspect this homeless person might have left that statement in your garage?"

A loud bang, wood smacking against wood, interrupted Anderson's reply. From beyond Kell's office door, the Chief caught the upset voice of his once-a-week-secretary, Marg Kenney, and then the clatter of someone stomping past her desk. "Sir! Sir, you can't go in there, the Chief is talking to someon—"

Noah burst into the room without knocking, pale-faced, his gray eyes giving off sparks.

Seeing him, knowing immediately why he must have come, lightning forked through Kell's gut. He tensed automatically, but he'd been expecting this, sooner or later. Of course, he'd hoped for later, after he'd had a little time to prepare the ground with prickly, independent Noah.

"Hey," he said. And he hoped that Noah didn't figure out how turned on he was right now, seeing him so pissy—he always wanted him, shy, responsive, angry—but he figured now was not the time to show it.

Noah slammed some wrapped-up diner food down on Kell's desk. "I can't believe I bought you lunch!"

111

"Whoa."

"We need to talk," Noah snapped.

"Agreed," Kell said. He stood, going to Noah and putting a gentle hand on his arm, practically feeling the passion sizzling through his skin. He cocked a brow at Anderson. "Why don't you grab lunch at the diner? We'll pick this up again."

The businessman glanced at Noah's stony face and looked uncomfortable, obviously picking up on the vibe. Tough shit. Kell knew folks figured he was bent, but now they'd have to get used to Kell being bent for Noah.

The man nodded. Seeing that his visitor would wait, Kell opened a side door into the file room, which was muffled by papers, and so better soundproofed than his office.

"What happened?" Though Kell had an idea.

"*You* happened. I told you in confidence about Adam and *he called me!* He said a police detective in Seattle asked him some questions." Noah swallowed, looking sick.

"Yes, I called a friend at the Seattle PD and I'd do it again," Kell admitted flatly.

"You had no right!"

"Wrong. Do you think you are the only man he ever frightened? I looked into his army records; he was dishonorably discharged after assaulting another man in the showers. He has a history, Noah, and I wanted to make my friend aware so he could do some digging."

"I trusted you, Kell, but I guess you just thought I was a coward, running away from Seattle, in need of someone's protection."

Kell shook his head. "Bull. What I know is you're pissed, but we're going to work it out." Noah growled under his breath, crossing his arms. "We are. And don't go putting words in my mouth that I think you're a coward." Kell took a deep breath. "I think maybe that's how you see *yourself*, but that's damn sure not what I see."

Noah's gaze fell, and he flushed, but Kell could see he was listening, at least.

"Looks like we need another mirror," Kell noted. "So you can see how incredibly brave I think you were, protecting your kid and listening to your instincts about a wrong guy." Feeling Noah still had to be rattled from that bastard's phone call, Kell struggled for a moment with his feelings of rage and possessiveness. He'd deal with Adam, oh, yes. For now though, there was Noah, and he needed Kell. "Sit down." Kell pointed to a chair. "Uh, please."

Noah cocked a wry brow but complied while Kell went to the coffee maker, filling up a mug and bringing it to Noah, kneeling beside him. "It's not fancy Seattle beans, but it's hot. Where's Josh?" he asked.

"At the library," Noah said, taking the peace offering and sipping from the mug. "I wanted to treat you to lunch, so I was in the diner when Adam—"

Kell's jaw flexed. "Baby, I'm sorry. I never meant for that son of a bitch to call you. I just wanted someone to look into his background. I wanted to make sure if he ever came to my town I knew who I was dealing with." He didn't add that he almost hoped Adam would come so he could have a piece of him. Maybe that wasn't responsible, but it was how he felt.

"But he's not your problem to deal with!" Noah shot back, putting down his coffee mug with a clatter on the nearest metal bookshelf.

Kell cupped Noah's cheek. "*Wrong,*" he said.

"Because I let you kiss me a couple of times and give me a hand job? That doesn't give you the right." Gray eyes snapped, but Kell could feel the cautious single dad still weighing him.

"Because I...." Kell swallowed, unable to continue for a moment, even knowing that if he wanted Noah, he'd have to give—

probably in every sense of the word. But his chest tightened when he thought of the burden of shame Noah still carried. Fuck! Adam was six three, heavily muscled. Noah was no match for that kind of man, trained to kill. He'd done the smart thing, following his gut.

"Kell."

"I was going to tell you about it but I wanted to give you some time to like me first," Kell admitted simply.

Noah rubbed his forehead. "I dealt with it."

"But you never let anyone close after it happened, did you?" Kell mulled.

"Not until you," Noah admitted, looking a little disgruntled. "But I was planning on dating again eventually, I'll have you know," he finished off huffily.

Kell caressed Noah's hair, waiting patiently, ready to listen.

"Okay, I admit, I wish I'd handled it differently!" Noah burst out.

"You were protecting Josh." Kell shook his head. "And you're right; you did handle it. Sometimes I almost wish…."

"What?"

"That I had someone like you when I was a kid."

Noah raised a weary hand, having had enough. "I don't want to talk about him anymore. I came here to make a fresh start. But I do like you, Kell."

"I want you to forget him," Kell agreed, his hand tender as he stroked Noah's curls, though his eyes were uncompromising. "But don't expect me to."

Noah pulled away. "Just what is it you want from me? I thought it was just something quick, like one night, but—"

"I don't know, but I can promise you one thing; it *won't* be quick," Kell answered, smiling as Noah's eyes widened. He wanted to banish the shadows now, for both of them. He bent close and glanced his lips against Noah's.

Noah shuddered, fingers gripping Kell's shoulders. "I'm still not sure of the wisdom of dating you. What does it entail?" Noah asked.

"Hmm, well, it means I get to take care of *this* for you." One big hand confidently reached down and gently squeezed Noah's stiffening sex through his jeans.

Noah leaned closer, his breath touching Kell's lips. "There's something to be said for cavemen sometimes."

"ARE you sure I can't convince you to head back?" Alec asked Jade as they crested another rise. They were deep in the woods above her house now, and Alec was gripping the talisman his grandmother had given him.

"Is that bit of voodoo doing any good?" Jade asked, wiping her sweaty face with a bandana and completely ignoring Alec's question. If he thought the little woman was staying put, he had a lot to learn about her. And she almost looked forward to teaching him.

But then she frowned at her own thoughts. Huh? She'd probably go back to barely being aware of him after this, and better for the Boy Scout if she did.

Alec shrugged. "Nothing yet." Then he frowned and paused to thrust some thorny runners from a blackberry bush carefully aside before kneeling next to the trail they were following. "Now that's something you don't see every day," he muttered.

"What?" Jade glanced around the moss-hung trees, jumpy. She'd never come up here growing up, and if her fool dog hadn't gone missing, she wouldn't be up here now. Not that she believed it was really a ghost or all that bullshit, but....

"I've seen these tracks before. Like someone with homemade moccasins or something." Alec pointed to a soft track in the mud.

"Huh." Jade didn't know anything about tracks, but it did look odd. "So someone's living rough up here?"

"Looks like there might be truth in the rumors since tracks don't lie. Whoever it is is very slim and in good shape, moving fast, as if they know the trails up here."

Jade liked how Alec talked to her, sharing the discovery as if she had a brain and not just a nice ass. She pushed her hair back, feeling the sweat on the back of her neck turning clammy in the chill of the damp forest.

"Do you think these tracks are also connected with what's going on lately?"

ALEC made a soft sound of agreement. "Everything is connected. I don't have to be my grandmother to see that." The bundle around his neck warmed, and he felt a corresponding tingle from the talisman his grandmother had given him. He straightened, senses on alert as he looked around. "Are you sure you want to keep going? We're going deeper into the forest than I've ever gone before."

"I really am worried about Beau," Jade said. "I remember flying over this stretch once. A real wilderness."

Alec tensed suddenly. He looked up into Jade's eyes and saw them widen.

"*Barking!*" Jade whispered, squeezing Alec's arm. "Alec, that sounded like Beau!"

AT THE library, Josh was lost in thought, his pencil scrawling random images and words on a pad of paper as he sifted through the impressions he'd had of the ghost that haunted the woods. He'd had a dream about him the night before, but when he woke up, his head was muddled and aching, and all he felt was... *grief.*

"Hey," the librarian, Mrs. Mathers, greeted Josh so he jumped and then huffed out an embarrassed laugh. The red-haired woman smiled at him. "You all right, Josh? Have you found everything you need?"

Josh shook his head, gaze on the stack of books he'd been going through, trying to work things out. "Not yet, but I will," he said.

"Hmm, a thoughtful young man. You remind me of a boy who used to come in here. He stopped a long time ago," Mrs. Mathers sighed.

Josh looked up at the older woman, seeing sadness in her eyes. "Is something wrong?"

She paused and chewed her lip. "For a long time, yes, I think something has been, Josh."

REGRETTING he couldn't mess around further with Noah in the file room—that was pushing it, even for Kell—he returned to his office with him. At least they'd cleared the air, and maybe he could talk him into another—he froze. "*Shit!*"

"What is it?"

"Anderson is gone and he helped himself to that lunch you brought me," Kell growled, annoyed; there had been a generous slice of peach pie in the mix. "So much for his fine manners." Kell strode through his office door. "Arlene!" he called to one of the county deputies doing paperwork at her borrowed space, giving him a hand with his overstretched beat. "Do a little more digging on Mr. Anderson, our local tycoon who was just in here."

"Yes, Chief!" the older woman nodded. "What all did he do?"

"He stole my lunch!" Kell said, outraged.

Noah smiled. "Come on, I'll buy you another," he offered.

Chapter 13

WYLDE buried his face in the dog's fur, warm for the moment. Sometimes the old retriever came and stayed with him in his shelter. It was the only creature that had been safe for him, hadn't chased him away after seeming to be his friend.

Wylde was desperate for the dog's affection, even as he knew that he'd soon be alone again, but the people were coming, and that was good. The dog had slipped, hurt himself.

"DO YOU feel that?" Jade whispered, grimacing and reaching out to put a hand on Alec's arm. "I pick it up sometimes—like we're being watched."

Alec didn't like it any more than Jade. He paused, closing his eyes and opening his senses. The night he and Kell had gone after Thomas, he'd experienced it, as if something watched from the forest. "I don't know exactly, but I think it might be connected to whatever is haunting these woods." He looked at her, reading her resolve. "We're almost at the first box canyon by my reckoning. It could be your dog got stuck there somehow."

Jade nodded. "Okay then. Let's get him out."

Alec took his shotgun from the scabbard that ran down his back. Sweat prickled his neck, pooling in the indentation above his collarbone. He'd be damned glad when he was back at the diner with Jade, with her trying to ignore him as usual while he gave her something to think about. Armed, he took point, stepping over deadfall carefully but keeping a wary eye on their back trail.

HALF an hour later, they reached sheer granite cliffs, the land looking like it had been sliced abruptly in a long vertical drop. Huffing, Alec leaned over the edge, studying the scrubby trees and pockets of sand on the slope. It was later afternoon, and since it was still springtime, the sun was declining rapidly, covered by clouds. "I think I can make it down there," he said, pointing to a chalky path in the rock face. "Maybe follow that."

"It's getting darker," Jade noted, pushing back brown hair tangled over her sweaty skin. She looked....

Alec swallowed and put it aside.

"I know. Take the flashlight and the gun and wait for me here," he ordered.

"Alec...." Jade thrust the flashlight into her jeans and gripped the gun he offered her, studying him, eyes wide. And suddenly it was so easy between them that he was leaning close, and then he was kissing her. When she didn't resist, their kiss ran long enough to leave him a little more breathless.

"Did you hear that?" Jade broke away to ask.

"More barking!" Alec pulled off his knapsack, readying himself for the climb. "Guess we're in the right place."

"I can't tell where it's coming from exactly; it's bouncing off the canyon walls." Jade frowned, examining the stained yellow, orange and reddish drop.

"Only one way to find out," he agreed. Alec took a deep breath, centering himself, gripping the talisman from his grandmother. His instincts whispered they were close to Jade's dog. And maybe something else....

"Wait!" Jade shucked her jean jacket, her mouth a stubborn line.

Guessing what she was up to, Alec shook his head. "Jade, you'll only slow me down."

"I'll only come part of the way. Come on, if we argue about it, we'll only lose more daylight!"

Alec gave in, since she was right; time, they didn't have. He went first, scrabbling down dirt and sand, pausing to help Jade navigate large chunks of scattered rock and debris. The warm spring air made him sweat freely.

"Looks like this path has been used before," Jade noted, looking up the trail they were following. "Who do you think uses it?"

"No idea, Jade. Be careful since there is no telling how stable it is," Alec warned.

"JOSH." Mrs. Mathers cocked a brow as she glanced at his collection of books, which was topped by a book about hauntings in the Pacific Northwest. "You don't really believe in a ghost on Sullivan's Mountain?"

Josh looked down at his books. "No, Ma'am. I just wanted to read up on all kinds of possibilities to eliminate what I think is going on." It helped to talk about his ideas with someone neutral. Lately, the stakes felt higher because of the new man in his dad's life, though he knew that was messed up and probably just him feeling like a kid.

She sat down beside him. "Don't you think you should confide in your father?" she asked gently.

Josh bit his lip. "I'm worried, but not just about myself. I think someone is maybe in trouble."

Josh looked up when he saw his father at the library door. He shoved his books into his duffle bag and smiled at the older woman. "I'll tell him, promise. Gotta go!"

ALEC and Jade finally reached a sandy crevice jutting out above the open arms of the canyon. The sun was a yellow spotlight, hitting the very top of the cliff now, setting fast, so that Jade skidded on a shadowed pile of debris. "Whew, we made it!" She caught Alec's gaze. "What's up?"

Alec pointed to the rubble, dried poplar saplings, cracked mud, and cedar branches. "Kind of looks like a rough shelter from this angle. You know, to keep out the rain?"

Jade's dark brows rose. "Yeah, really crude. Kind of Anasazi now you point it out."

"Yeah, if it weren't getting dark fast I'd take a closer look."

Alec retrieved the flashlight and shone the beam into the crack in the cliff.

"*Beau!*" Jade ran to her aging golden retriever, who whined, thumping his feathery tail. His body was lodged under a heavy log, possibly from a fall down the treacherous path above.

"Trapped," Alec muttered. "We'll have to free him."

"Alec, I can't lift this on my own!" Jade rasped, face shiny as she strained.

"Wait for me." Alec hastened over to Jade. "We can't stay long, or we'll have a hell of a walk back up that path. It's slippery," he said.

"I don't plan on it!" Jade pulled as Alec put his back into helping her free her dog. They tugged together, hands scrabbling for purchase.

From the cliff above, pebbles fell, spattering like rain.

Hushed, Alec ordered, "Better hold the gun while I find a log or something to use as leverage to free Beau, Jade."

"SAY again?" Kell barked on his radio. The static in the diner was a killer. He was also disappointed at the interruption from a nice late meal with Noah and Josh. And damn it, he hadn't had his slice of peach pie yet! He'd taken up running again after chasing over the mountain paths, so he figured he could have burned the calories off.

"Alec's grandmother Ruth just called, Chief," county deputy Arlene Falco was saying. "She said Alec and Jade needed help and you should head up to the first box canyon above her house."

"Roger!" Kell looked at Noah. "Well, hell."

"Lawman's hours, I know."

"Do you?" Kell hoped so. "It's usually a pretty sleepy town." What he didn't add was he hadn't been Chief long before he'd learned to listen to Alec's grandmother. He didn't necessarily believe she had special powers or anything, but she'd put him on the right trail a time or two.

"And I hope it will be again soon, a sleepy town, I mean. I'm sure you'll make sure of it."

Reluctantly, Kell climbed to his feet and then glanced at Josh, who was studying his books, as if wanting to give them a moment. The kid was tactful, he had to give him that, and apparently working to be approving of an unconventional friendship for his father.

"I'll have coffee waiting for you when you get home." Then Noah flushed at the slip. "I mean at our house, of course."

Kell's eyes warmed. "I like what you called it the first time." In front of God and everyone in the diner, he kissed Noah on the lips. "Have to go." Kell put his hat on. "Oh, and since I'm staying with you, I'll need a key. I really don't want to wake you up if I'm late."

Noah dug a brass one out of his shopping bag. "I had one cut first thing this morning. And I bought free range eggs."

"Son of a bitch!" Then Kell flushed, giving Josh a sheepish look over his swearing. He guessed he'd have to watch that from now on. "Uh, I mean, does this mean real eggs for breakfast?"

Noah glanced around at the fascinated townsfolk. "Kell," he said in an undertone. "Shouldn't you be more discreet?"

Kell shrugged on his jacket and groped for the keys to his truck. He figured he'd use the road they'd cut into the woods for logging as a shortcut to the canyon to look for Alec and Jade.

"I had my fill of keeping things secret in the army. And I'm proud to date you, Noah," Kell said flatly.

NOAH watched the Chief stride from the room, still searching his pockets absently, as if looking for his keys.

He swallowed the sudden lump in his throat and looked at Josh.

"He's definitely a keeper, Dad," Josh approved, arching a saucy brow.

THE slope was in deep shadow now and freezing, fully exposed to the dusk air. Jade listened to the sound of her own heart pounding as she waited for Alec to return; he'd headed further down the slope in search of something to use to pry Beau free.

She couldn't wait to get out of here, though thank God no more pebbles had showered down, freaking her out with the creepy feeling they weren't alone. After finding Morley Orris, it was not something she really wanted to experience.

"Hang on, honey," she whispered to her dog. "Alec will be right back. He's a pretty good guy, even, you know, with all the testosterone making him crazy; just don't tell him I told you that."

Beau suddenly stiffened under Jade's hand, golden eyes fixed on their back trail.

"*What?*" she whispered, dread making her grip the shotgun tighter. "You hear somethin'?"

Jade peered into the darkness above but couldn't make out whatever it was her dog sensed.

Beau whined before putting his head down on his paws. Jade told herself she was imagining that her dog looked sad.

"YOU okay, Josh?" Noah asked as they drew up at the house. He smiled when he took in their extra passenger, a rescue Sheltie sitting sedately on Josh's lap. Her name was Fiona, and as soon as they'd walked into the breeder's log cabin after their late meal with Kell, she'd walked over to Josh, as if to say she'd been expecting him.

From there, Noah had settled the business part, still a little dazed at how much he needed to know to properly adopt a dog. They would have to go shopping soon for all kinds of paraphernalia.

"I'm okay, Dad." Josh looked up, arms wrapped around Fiona. "Guess we better get her a crate for the truck, huh?"

"We'll have to drive to a larger town for that, Josh, but I can spare some time from the edits of my latest textbook tomorrow." His brow wrinkled. "Are you sure you're okay? Those books you picked up at the library...."

Josh flushed. "You don't think someone is lost in the woods? Like, how I would be if suddenly you weren't there anymore."

Noah wanted to dismiss Josh's fears and put them into perspective, and he'd have done just that except... except something *was* happening on Sullivan's Mountain, and sensitive Josh had picked up on it, maybe because he was feeling vulnerable with the changes in his dad's life. And Kell was worried.

"I think it's very unlikely. Josh, you are the most important person in my life. If you were ever lost, I would look for you, find you." Noah sighed. "Maybe I should show you again all the security I had installed for the house and grounds." Seeing Josh bury his face in the Sheltie's fur, Noah continued, "I know the house is kind of ugly, but I tried to make it safe for you."

Josh nodded. "I guess I didn't want to tell you how I'm feeling on edge. Dumb, huh?"

Noah brushed his son's shoulder. "I'm glad you did. Just remember that secrets have a way of coming out, sometimes when we least want them to. Now do you think we should give Fiona a bath? She'll just fit in the kitchen sink."

Josh surprised Noah by unbuckling his seatbelt and hugging him, something he rarely did anymore at twelve, the Sheltie squirming a bit, annoyed to be crushed between father and son. "I know the Chief is trying to get to the bottom of stuff. I only hope he can."

"We'll all do our part, Josh." Noah realized after he made the promise that he'd referred to himself and Kell as a unit. "You just have to trust us."

"I'll try, Dad."

Noah stretched over to Josh's seat and gingerly removed the abandoned blanket after his son left their Tundra. He had a feeling he'd be doing a lot of cleaning up in the future, but they'd gotten microfiber on the furniture precisely so they could make this adjustment.

"*Dad?*"

Noah stiffened at the fear in Josh's voice. He dropped the blanket, shoved the door open and strode after his son.

"Josh?"

A familiar big man with dark hair in his eyes and olive brown smiling eyes was slouching in the alcove by the front door, giving Josh a charming smile. "Hey, kid, you miss me?"

"*No,*" Josh growled, holding Fiona in a protective stance.

Noah felt like someone had punched him in the chest.

Adam.

Chapter 14

ALEC strained, gritting his teeth. "Hear anything while I was gone?" he huffed, eying Jade as she stood sentinel. "Hey, keep that gun ready!"

"I've got it." Jade scowled, hefting the shotgun. "Trust me."

"You better, baby," Alec growled.

Jade took a deep breath, as if reining in her exasperation. "Yes, I do, and nope, nothing since earlier. That's a good sign, right?" Her dark eyes studied the shadowed cliff. "And anyway... Beau doesn't seem worried."

Since the bundle was hot against his sweaty skin, signaling something off, Alec didn't answer but continued shoving with a half-rotten poplar sapling, using it under the log that held Jade's distressed golden retriever to try to pry the animal free.

Crack!

"*Fuck!*" Alec staggered back, slamming a fist against rock. The sapling had snapped in his hands, and now a cold finger poked his spine. To find this one, he'd been gone about twenty minutes. Now....

"Jade, I have to try again to find something to use as a lever." Alec resisted the urge to kick the shattered wood. Truth was, he was a little scared. Scared of whatever the fuck was haunting the woods that might have killed Morley Orris, scared to leave the woman he loved alone to possibly face it. "I'll… have to go further down, deeper into the forest below."

"Okay." Jade swallowed visibly, her face ghostly in the glow of the flashlight, freckles standing out and pupils dilated. "Beau and I will be okay until you find the right thing."

Abruptly the pouch around Alec's neck was a steady warmth, not quite as hot, as if whatever menaced them had moved away. So they had more time, didn't they?

"I'll be back as soon as I can." Thinking he had nothing to lose, Alec kissed her surprised lips. "Try not to make any noise. And take care of yourself for me."

Jade shoved the flashlight into his hands. "You'll need that to find your way."

Alec stared at her, loath to leave her. "Don't shoot me when I come back, okay?"

Jade's eyes were wide and frightened, but she only nodded jerkily. "Right. If I see a flashlight, don't shoot. If I see something else…."

Alec's lips firmed into a hard line. "Shoot to kill."

"JOSH, go in the house," Noah heard himself order in a calm voice. He almost wanted to laugh, thinking what a fraud he was. He'd moved here, all the way down here to this near-wilderness, to avoid this man. He swallowed thickly, riding the raft of emotion of seeing Adam again. *Think of Josh. You have to take care of him. Nothing else matters.*

"Dad."

He looked at his son, seeing fear in the eyes so like his own. "Don't worry."

Josh glared at Adam but then slammed past him, obediently entering their house. Noah breathed a sigh of relief even as he spotted his son a moment later, staring through the window of the great room at them, his Blackberry in hand. He was sorry that Fiona's homecoming had been shadowed; they'd looked forward to it, planned for it as part of moving down here.

"How did you find me?" Noah couldn't believe he sounded so reasonable. Was this the man he'd lived in fear of? Brown eyes, brown hair, so pedestrian. For a moment, he felt like he was an actor in a melodramatic play. Had he really left Seattle because he was so uneasy to encounter him again?

"I run a security company. Figure it out!" Adam said, giving Noah a familiar indulgent look.

Noah gritted his teeth, nodding tightly. "And that's how you got my number, even though very few people have it. I assume this is over Chief Farraday contacting a detective in Seattle about you?"

Adam shifted so his broad, thickly muscled body stood between Noah and the refuge of his house. He leaned forward, smiling slightly and whispering, "I would have tracked you down sooner or later."

"Why?" Noah wanted to take a step back, creeped out, but he knew it would be a mistake with this man.

Adam's eyes widened. "What do you mean? I had a thing for you. It's not over just because you got a little skittish."

Noah stared at Adam. Could the man be that stupid? "You made me very uncomfortable. Do you think I'd ever let you treat me that way again?"

Adam shook his head. "Look, I know I have some problems with my temper but I dated you a long time, Noah, and I never pushed things until that night. And then all I fucking did was hold you pressed against me. I don't know why that was such a big deal!"

Noah laughed bitterly, remembering the sound of his own heart beating in his ears as Adam put a hand around his throat. His touch had been light, but Noah had felt something shift between them. "Damn right you didn't push things, or I would have stopped seeing you!"

"I could never stop thinking about you," Adam drawled, leaning against the porch support. "The one that got away."

"Not my problem." Noah's face felt tight, like a mask. Was this truly him speaking, this strong, defiant man, standing up to Adam? "After that last night I took steps to learn how to defend myself."

As if to test Noah's words, Adam suddenly lunged. In reaction, Noah struck the larger man's forearms, *hard,* the months of training making him react instinctively. He was rewarded when Adam's eyes widened in surprise. "Some martial arts training, I grant you, but I could take you," Adam scoffed.

"No, you're right. I can't fight you and win," Noah admitted, falling back, retracing his steps to his Tundra.

"Noah, I just want to talk to you. It's not like you were seeing anyone after you stopped taking my calls."

"How do you know that?" Again, that brush of wrong. "I don't want to talk to you, Adam." Noah opened the trunk, keeping his face carefully schooled as he reached into a rectangular box he'd made Josh swear he'd never touch, pulling free the shotgun and pointing it toward Adam's feet, ready to level it if he had to.

"Whoa!"

"You came here because you got wind someone was investigating you, fine, but I want you gone," Noah growled. "I learned how to use this for protection when we decided to move down here."

"You wouldn't shoot me." Adam held up his hands. "You're not a killer, Noah. I know the type."

"*I would.* Right through the chest and a second one to the belly. The retired Navy Seal who taught me how to use this gun said it's good to hit the body in two different places if you want to bring a man down." Noah cocked a brow. "Don't push me, Adam."

Adam's eyes narrowed. "You told that Chief about me, didn't you? You couldn't face me like a man, so you put him on my trail as soon as you thought you were safe."

Noah shook his head. "Believe what you like. Now I want you gone; this is my place now." His voice was firm, as if it came from a place rooted in the ground he was standing firm on, his pulse racing and his palms sweaty, but there was a still, singing rightness inside. He would kill Adam if push came to shove. Kill in a heartbeat to protect himself and his son.

"SHIT!" Alec shoved the branch aside in disgust. It was wet and broke easily in his hands, half-rotten like the rest. He had to find something more than deadfall! He looked up at a towering Douglas fir, branches moving in the cold breeze like arms reaching out, and in the flashlight's circle made out a branch about the size he needed a mere ten feet above the ground, tantalizing him.

This had already taken too fucking long! He needed to get back to Jade and Beau.

Deciding to go for it, he placed the flashlight where it would shine up the tree, ripped his T-shirt, the sound loud in the sleeping woods, and wrapped his hands.

Then he put a foot to the bottom of the tree and reached up for the first branch.

"UH, COME on, *come on!*" Alec was twisting the branch he'd zeroed in on when his medicine pouch stung his skin in abrupt warning.

He froze, heart pounding, suspended, peering beyond the faint lemon glow from his flashlight to the woods beyond.

BEAU was barking!

"Oh, Jesus, this isn't good!" Jade muttered to herself. Alec had been gone for what seemed like forever, and now her dog was acting fierce all of a sudden. She gripped the shotgun tighter, glad that Alec had left it, even as she was frightened for him.

Beau growled again, brown eyes staring beyond Jade. "*Beau, be quiet!*" she shushed her dog, but then Jade had had it! Had it with being scared and had it with not taking direct action, which was not like her. She reached for the broken sapling Alec had abandoned, shoving it under the debris holding her dog fast. She pushed, feeling a muscle tearing in her back; this was far beyond her strength, but still she strained—

Beau suddenly bounded free, wasting no time in plastering his body against Jade's, trembling as they huddled against each other under starlight, listening.

She made out the faint scrabble of stones. Footsteps! Alec returning, or something else...?

ALEC worked, frantic, and finally the branch snapped, a decisive sound, loud as the crack of a gunshot in the hushed quiet of the forest. He let it fall, watching as it hit the ground, olive colored needles shuddering. Panting, he backhanded the sweat from his forehead.

The bundle was a steady warning heat against his skin, prodding him, and then he caught it, something moving fast through the brush toward him, making nearby blackberry bushes shiver in its passage.

Suddenly the flashlight rolled an arc, shoved aside by…?

Alec caught his first look as a figure sprang easily into the tree opposite where he sheltered. Black, rough-cut hair, almost down to a browned waistline, wide blue eyes full of fear and curiosity… dirty hands with a grip on the branches.

"Holy shit!" Alec whispered.

"*DON'T shoot!*"

Jade lowered the gun, huffing for breath. "Holy-fucking-*hell!*" she muttered, trembling.

"Don't be afraid, young lady," Mr. Anderson admonished. Jade immediately recognized the older man, squint lines burned deep into his skin surrounding pale gray eyes, though she'd only met him once or twice at the Anderson house. He was holding a flashlight, thank heavens, and Jade was glad for the light.

Jade stood, back sore and protesting, holding onto her dog so he didn't do something stupid like run off into the deeper forest, since retrievers could be the dumb blonds of dogdom. "I'm not afraid and I'm no lady, or so your wife made clear. No offense, but what the heck are you doing down here in this canyon?"

The older man dropped the light so it focused its glare on the ground between them. "Would you mind not pointing that gun in my direction?" he asked, very mildly.

Jade raised her brows. "Soon as I feel comfortable you're not moonlighting as some weird-ass-ghost-impersonating-serial-killer, yeah, I'll be sure to do that."

"You know very well I'm a successful businessman, so I do deals, not people," the older man reassured her.

"Deals, huh?" Jade blinked, gun up and fixed on her former employer as he picked his way toward the edge of the shelf where she'd been huddling with her dog. Finally she shrugged, letting her gun hand fall. "Just in case you don't remember me, I'm Jade. And I do men, mostly."

ALEC had one moment of holding wide, frightened eyes, his sweaty wrapped palms slipping—

And then he was falling.

Chapter 15

AN SUV suddenly careened into Noah's driveway, parking crookedly. Next thing, a rumpled, unshaven, and cranky-looking Kell Farraday erupted out of the vehicle.

Noah didn't take his eyes off Adam, knowing better, but he felt like cheering, guessing that Josh must have summoned Kell.

Adam had his hands up, watching Kell approach him, clearly recognizing another predator. In contrast, Kell's big body bristled like a protective Doberman's confronting a trespasser.

"He's fucking you? Well, that explains why the Chief of this hick town would have looked me up," Adam noted, eyes reading Kell. "Isn't that right, Noah?"

HEART pounding at the close call, since he'd been on his way up the steep logging road when he caught Josh's call for help, Kell was fucking relieved to find Noah safe. More than safe; it looked like he was handling the situation. Still, Kell was glad to be here, and fortunately, another deputy was already on site at the top of the canyon to start the search for Alec and Jade, so Kell had been free to burn rubber and divert straight to Noah's house.

Now he took a deep breath, reading the situation with the experience of a man who had commanded men. He studied Noah out of the corner of his eye, the competent way he gripped the gun, his set expression, and Kell recognized that his formerly timid lover had come a long way in dealing with his fears.

Kell came to a sudden, lightning decision on how to play this out. He folded his arms and strode closer to Adam, ready to take him if he pushed things, but he didn't order Noah to put away his shotgun.

"No," Kell said clearly, wanting to tear out the other man's throat but more than willing to humiliate him first. "Noah fucks *me.*"

"YOU didn't happen to see my friend Alec anywhere? I'm not alone up here," Jade clarified, frowning. "He's way overdue gettin' back to me and he's not the kind of guy to ditch a girl. Just don't tell him I said that."

Mr. Anderson shone a light at a tall figure just broaching the heights where they were standing. "This friend, perhaps?"

"*ALEC!*"

Alec wasn't prepared for the bullet that struck him, full to the chest. A Jade-bullet made up of her slender, compactly muscled body and long brown hair.

"Shit, careful!" he begged, rubbing the bloody wound on his forehead.

Her retriever was somehow free, he was relieved to notice, whining and sniffing Alec, as if catching a familiar scent. He rubbed the goose egg again, shaking his head, still groggy, a little sick; it was a fucking miracle he'd staggered back up the slope at all, but he'd been worried about Jade. "Sorry I took so long getting back. I must have passed out."

"I was so going to look for you!" Jade scolded, stroking his hair. He decided he rather liked that. "Did you fall and hurt yourself? Are you okay?"

"Head hurts. I just took a spill from a tree." Alec recognized Mr. Anderson. The hell...? "Funny finding you out here, sir." He managed to firm his shaky voice.

Jade gave the older man an unreadable look. "He scared the shit out of me, showing up out of the dark!" She paused after looking Alec over. "Alec, don't be proud. Let me help you." Jade steadied him, strong from the weights he knew she lifted at the local gym. How often had he gone there himself and worked out, watching her?

"Thanks. Sorry I couldn't rescue you," he apologized, chagrined. Way to capture a lady's heart.

"That's okay." Jade's lips quirked, though her dark eyes were full of concern, so he couldn't help but be slightly heartened. "I'm not really the wait to be rescued type, in case you haven't noticed."

Alec nodded. "I noticed. My heroine."

"We shouldn't linger, I don't think," Mr. Anderson interrupted. He was studying something in the mud by the shelter they'd discovered.

"What is it? Did you find something?" Alec rasped.

With Jade's arm around him, he went over to see what the businessman had found. "Tracks."

"I wager you know who left them, young man. Possibly the same person who stole my missing gun," Mr. Anderson noted, very gently. "You've *seen* him, haven't you?"

Alec shook his head. "No idea what you mean, sir."

"I don't believe you!" Anderson scoffed.

"You say you're looking for a missing gun? Is this the one your son lost?"

"Adopted son, yes." Anderson's mouth tightened. "I was fond of it. It's a collector's piece."

"Uh huh. So you are so desperate to find it, you're out here at night?"

"You're one to talk," Anderson said. "And it wasn't night when I set out."

ON THE way up the slope, Jade gripped Alec's hand. "You saw something, didn't you?"

Alec's mouth tightened. "Not now."

Sensing she was about to explode like summer lightning, Alec interjected some humor to head her off before she rained Jade-mood all over him. "I saw something, but it didn't stop to eat me. It's all good, Jade."

Jade's eyes narrowed. "It's not all good, but you're hurt, so you get a free one this time."

HANDS still up, Adam paused by Kell as he headed back to his rental car. "I understand you were an Army Ranger," he noted.

Kell's eyes narrowed, and a message seemed to pass between the two men. He gave a slight nod and then watched as Adam climbed into his car and drove away.

Noah let the shotgun fall. He wiped his mouth with trembling fingers. "I thought you were supposed to tell me to drop my weapon or something," he challenged Kell.

Kell shrugged. "You had it covered. If I thought you couldn't deal with him, I would have taken it from you," he said flatly.

Noah's eyes snapped at Kell's explanation, even as he acknowledged to himself it was just common sense on the part of a lawman. The point was, Kell had decided Noah *was* handling himself.

Josh appeared, Blackberry still in hand. He gave a little smile when he saw Noah and Kell standing so close together, as if picking up on the silent support flowing between them. Picking up on it and approving of it.

"You called the Chief," Noah said.

His son nodded and then, after hesitating a moment, went to his dad, hugging him. "I didn't want him to hurt you."

Noah's eyes widened. "Josh."

He looked at Kell accusingly, but Kell put his hands up, shaking his head. "Hey, I didn't tell him anything, but like I've said before, he's a smart kid."

"You sure told him off, Dad!" Josh crowed. "He went totally white when you had the drop on him."

Kell reached out and took the shotgun from Noah's shaking hand. He checked it, finding it loaded and ready to rock. Noah hadn't been bluffing about shooting Adam, he noted with satisfaction.

He looked at Noah, letting the appreciation show in his eyes. "You sure did, Noah," he agreed softly.

Noah closed his eyes, and Kell saw immediately he needed a moment. "Josh? I want to talk to your Dad alone."

Josh gave Noah a worried look. "It's harder not knowing stuff," he told his father.

Noah's eyes widened at what Josh was implying. "You're right, of course. We'll talk in a little while, if you want. All right?" He wasn't sure how much he'd share with his son, but enough so that Josh wouldn't feel he was cut out of his father's life anymore. Josh was handling his father's orientation all right, and Noah didn't want any more secrets to come between them. That was the real reason he'd come here, wanted a fresh start.

And ironically, hadn't he told Josh just before Adam appeared that secrets had a way of showing up at your door?

His son nodded, satisfied. "Okay. But don't totally try to protect me, Dad. I can handle myself too."

When Josh was out of sight, Kell took Noah gently in his arms. "I'm sorry, baby. He was never supposed to know I'd talked to you. He must have a source at the Seattle PD. Guess it makes sense in his business."

"*God!* I was…!" Noah shook his head.

"Scared, yeah, but you held your ground."

"With your help."

"You didn't need me, and I want you to remember that." Kell kissed Noah firmly on the lips. "I'm sorry that I can't stay, be a proper boyfriend, but I was driving around the back roads, looking for signs of Alec and Jade, when Josh rang me."

"A proper boyfriend, huh? *Go.* I'll be all right." Noah's fingers were tangled with Kell's.

"I know you will." Kell cupped Noah's cheeks and nuzzled his lips tenderly against him. It felt so intimate that Noah's throat constricted. Boyfriend. He guessed Kell was.

As Kell climbed into his SUV, Noah couldn't resist teasing him, cocking an eyebrow and calling, "*I'm fucking you?*"

Kell flushed. "I wanted him to know you were strong. To a man like that, topping means you're strong."

"Uh huh," Noah said, deciding if he could take on Adam, he was more than ready to take on Kell. "And I think I like the idea."

Kell looked nervous. "Uh… we'll talk about it. Sometime."

HALF an hour after leaving Noah's driveway, Kell brought his truck to a halt as he spotted Jade walking with Alec on one of the old tree-sprouting builders' roads. She had her arm around the deputy, and her dog also limped by her side.

"Well, hell. What happened?" he demanded as soon as he opened his door.

"Oh man. I got a hell of a headache, Chief. Ask Mr. Anderson," Alec complained.

Kell looked around. "How would I do that? He's nowhere around."

Alec shrugged. "Must have ditched us. Sorry I couldn't take him in for stealing your lunch."

"I'll grant you asylum this once, on account you look like you couldn't take on a bunny rabbit with both hands." Kell helped Alec into the truck. In an undertone for the deputy's ears only, he added, "You sure you're okay?"

"Just need some Tylenol. Possibly half a bottle," Alec muttered. "I'm really sorry I didn't keep track of Anderson, Chief. One minute he was there…."

"Yeah," Kell said. "I'd really like to know what he was doing up here." He looked at Jade, who had been content merely to take in the interaction so far. "Glad you found your dog, Ms. Jade."

"Thanks to Alec," she said, settling against him.

Kell's eyes widened and then twinkled as he took in Alec's blush. Uh huh. Looked like more had gone down on the mountain than a hunt for Jade's dog. Well, it was about time. Alec had only been in love with her for years.

Kell started the engine, holding Alec's gaze in the rearview mirror as his face sobered. "Any sign of anyone else?"

Alec blew out a breath. "Yeah, you could say that."

"You saw someone?"

"Yep."

"So?"

"So we have a problem, Chief."

Chapter 16

NOAH had been expecting Kell to check up on him as soon as he was free, and he wasn't disappointed when the Chief appeared with Deputy Alec Danvers a couple of hours later on the undulating patio surrounding his lagoon pool. In the discreet illumination provided by his landscaping, he noticed Alec was sporting a white plaster bandage on his forehead, but his mouth was set in determined lines, making Noah wonder if Kell had filled him in on Adam's visit to the house.

"Gentlemen, I was just relaxing," Noah said, stepping free of the purple hot tub and reaching for a towel. Studying the two lawmen, he couldn't help but notice Kell's appreciative long look. "I hope Jade is all right?"

Alec nodded, looking pleased at the question. "She's fine. Thanks for asking."

"Well, so am I. Fine, I mean," Noah said, holding Kell's sharp and concerned gaze. "It's late, so are you, um, back for the night?" He flushed at what Alec might make of that question.

Kell put his hands on his hips. "I'm glad to hear that and no, there's something I need to do, but I thought I'd drop by and see if you wanted me to pick up some steaks down at the market before they close." Kell's eyes lightened as he brought the topic to shallow waters.

Noah shook his head. "I'm making a veggie stir fry for a late dinner. It's very healthy."

"I'm sure. No meat?" Kell asked plaintively.

"*No,*" Noah replied, although he was already considering it. Damn it, look what having a boyfriend did to an orderly man's life! "You can always eat somewhere else, I suppose."

Kell shook his head with mock sadness. "Only one table I want to put my feet under, and that's yours."

"YOU don't have to stay here with me. I *am* fine," Noah told Alec after Kell left. They were in Noah's kitchen while he chopped up vegetables for the dinner he planned to provide. And all right, he did have some lean steak he was planning on adding especially for Kell; he wanted to surprise him. He guessed that was also boyfriend territory, though in some ways he was groping his way as much as Kell.

Alec shook his head, leaning against the counter and sipping the fine Seattle coffee Noah had made him with apparent relish. "Kell didn't tell me much, but he wanted to make sure you weren't left alone until Adam is on his way out of town."

Noah stared at Alec, realization hitting him like a tree hitting the ground.

Alec muttered, "Oops."

"Kell's gone to find Adam?" Noah grabbed a dishtowel and dried his hands. "That sneaky barbarian!"

"Whoa, I don't want to get into Kell's business," Alec said gravely, putting aside his coffee. "But I think he really cares about you."

"He doesn't need to behave like a caveman to show me that!" Noah growled.

Alec looked like he was fighting a smile. "Caveman, huh? Don't worry, Noah. The Chief just wanted to exchange a few firm words with your ex."

"But Alec, can't you see that because he's a lawman, he can't brawl with Adam!" Noah pulled off his apron. "It's just not done."

Alec shook his head. "I guess it's done here. And he's not just a lawman; he's *your* man. What else can he do?"

"He can be something other than a small town cliché. Aren't you concerned?" Noah snatched his keys from the pocket of his pants. "Adam is a very formidable man!"

Alec shrugged, not looking very worried. "I just know Kell."

"I wondered why Adam left so easily!" Noah muttered. "Where did they arrange to meet?"

KELL closed the door of Al's Road House behind him. This time of night only Daisy and Madras, the owners, were around… along with one stranger to their town.

Adam.

Pushing his silky brown hair out of his eyes with well-manicured fingers, the big man stood up from the bar as Kell approached.

Madras put up his hands, obviously feeling the heavy atmosphere. "Fellas…."

"I'll cover any damages, Madras," Kell told the gray-eyed and string-figured barkeep softly. How often had he come here as a deputy himself and broken up a fight on Saturday nights? He took off his shield and his gun and placed them both on the bar. "It okay if we go outside?" It would be better if they got down to business in the woods out back instead of a public place.

"As long as I get to watch, Kell!" Madras laughed. "No way I'd miss this."

Kell shook his head, rueful. "Hold onto my personal items for me?"

KELL took a deep breath, taking off his wristwatch and watching Adam do the same. He sized him up as the Seattle man next removed his shirt, revealing a deep chest, furry with hair, heavily muscled.

In contrast, Kell was lighter-bodied, his chest smooth. *Was this really a good idea?* he wondered as he pulled off the T-shirt he'd worn under his uniform shirt. He spent most of his time trying to talk drunken lunkheads out of settling their disputes with their fists... but this, this was different.

Adam had frightened Noah, and no one had been there to protect him. Kell could never go back in time and do it, but he could stand up here, now. Make sure Adam knew how things stood in his town.

Besides, he thought as he shook out his arms, loosening up, he understood Adam; they were both warriors, both trained to fight.

And Noah was worth it. Worth bruises or broken teeth. Worth being patient and hoping he'd show up one night in Kell's bedroom.

NOAH strode inside the roadhouse, blinking at the smoky haze as his eyes adjusted. He saw a man and a woman with their arms folded, standing attentively, watching something through the dusty picture windows at the back of the tavern. Guessing what it might be, Noah hurried to join them.

"Oh, no," Noah murmured when he caught a glimpse. Shirt off, chest heaving, and sporting a bleeding cut over one eye, Kell evaded a kick from Adam, who was also stripped down.

Both men were panting for breath, obviously having been at this for a while; they circled each other, looking for an opening.

145

Noah's chest tightened. *Kell!* He was so much smaller than towering Adam, and although he'd belonged to an elite branch of the military, so had Adam.

"Noah say my name when you put it to him?" Adam taunted, as if seeking to anger Kell and shake him from his game.

"He doesn't usually say words… just a lot of moaning, and 'oh yeah, baby, *more!*'" Kell smirked.

Lightning fast, Adam struck Kell's raised forearms. The hard smack of impact made Noah clench his fists. *Oh, God, keep Kell safe.* He flashed back to what it felt to be helpless, crushed close by Adam, feeling sick.

Adam punched Kell, making him reel. He followed up with another wallop, not giving him time to recover. He swatted him again… and *again!*

Kell's leg swung out, and Adam leaped back to avoid it, but he swayed for a moment, and Kell caught him from behind, sinewy tanned arm around his neck as he punched Adam twice to the kidney.

In retaliation, Adam rammed his elbow back, but Kell had already danced away, his eyes holding Adam's as they circled again, hungry to tear into each other.

"I think the little bitch talks too much. Why else did you look into my background?"

"First…." Kell swung, and Adam dodged, but Kell followed it up with a wicked uppercut, slamming the other man's chin hard enough to make him bite his tongue so blood frothed from his lips. "Noah is not *anyone's* bitch. He would have drilled you if you tried to hurt him or his son. You're fucking lucky I came along when I did and rescued you."

Adam's eyes were a flat mud color, primitive in that moment. He rocked back before feinting another attack. Struggling with Kell, lips scraping back over bared teeth, arms locked, he smashed the

Chief head first into a picnic table, knocking aside an old tin ashtray full of abandoned butts.

Kell's head fell back, dripping blood from a gash, and he dropped, snagging one of Adam's thick legs and using his weight to throw the other man into some stained ivory plastic chairs.

As Noah watched, breathing fast, narrowed eyes burning, gut tight, both men sprang to their feet, blood running freely now.

"HE DOESN'T need me to protect him. Not from you," Kell rasped. Shit, he was hurting! But Adam could deliver all the hurt he could offer—Kell would never back down.

"So why take me on, Boy Scout?" Adam jeered, spitting blood. "Unless you're afraid he'll go back to me. What can a hick like you offer a man like Noah?"

"Because you scared him once. Because I want you gone. And Noah seems to like my edges," Kell said, enjoying the extra emphasis on the last word. He could see that Adam caught his inference.

"The little bitch teased me."

Kell swung, and Adam evaded, before pile-driving Kell in the jaw with a right cross.

Kell blinked, dizzy, his vision shaking. A second later, instinctively he ducked, and Adam missed landing his next punch.

Snarling, Kell went for the body. He was smaller, lighter on his feet, and he figured Adam was used to the advantages of his greater reach, height and power. He might not have the stamina to take the pain and keep going—

Kell hit low to the gut, slamming an elbow just above Adam's groin into his bladder before striking with stiff fingers into the center of the big man's chest.

Adam's eyes widened, and he wheezed, instinctively panicking when his lungs struggled for air.

Merciless and driven by cold, focused rage, Kell swung a smooth back kick, striking the other man in the collar bone. A little higher and he would have smashed Adam's windpipe, killing him, but he wasn't trying to kill… not quite.

He wanted to *hurt.*

Adam toppled, his body heavy as a felled Western Red Cedar as he crashed to the packed earth.

Kell knelt and locked both arms around Adam's neck while Adam panted to breathe, helpless. One satisfying twist and Kell could break his neck. Blood ran down his face, and he fought his instinctive need to do that. To kill as he had when he was a soldier, to take out this threat once and for all….

"*Kell, don't!*" And then Noah was there. Cupping Kell's sweaty cheek, ignoring Adam, who dropped from Kell's arms like a broken doll.

"He *hurt* you," Kell gasped, his body battered from the punishment he'd taken, but his blood was singing, so he felt like he could do anything, conquer anyone.

"He's nothing," Noah said calmly, as if knowing he had to reach Kell. "Thank you for helping me see that." Noah tugged Kell to his feet, putting an arm around him to steady him.

Kell looked down at Adam, who glared hate at him. "He's not a cocktease with the *right* man," Kell said.

"HONEY, I think it might be a couple of days before I can chase you around the room," Kell groaned as Noah helped him carefully back into his SUV. Noah had abandoned his own Tundra for the moment, since it was clear that Kell was hurting too much to drive himself.

"You *caveman!*" Noah slammed into his seat on the driver's side. "What the hell was that supposed to prove? He could have killed you!"

Kell blinked, wiping the blood from his eyes. "You care about me, Noah."

"No, I'm *pissed* at you! Pay attention!" Noah huffed. "Rock for brains, primitive, he-man, hick, barbarian—"

"*I am,*" Kell said, looking smug. "I am paying attention, Noah. Adam said you'd never go for a guy like me."

Noah paused, hands working the wheel. After a moment, he looked at Kell, who was dripping blood on the dark charcoal car upholstery, who had a large shiner expanding around one eye like an exploding nebula, who was looking at Noah like he was his North Star.

Hoarsely, he admitted, "I don't want to lose you now I've found you."

"I knew you'd take to me," Kell crowed. He lifted one battered fist in a victory sign. "*Yes!*"

Noah muttered more words in an undertone as he pulled free of the tavern's parking lot.

"You think we could swing by the twenty-four hour market for a steak?" Kell asked, holding his sore eye.

"No," Noah said flatly.

"No?" Kell gave him a sad look.

"No, we don't need to. I stocked up on eggs, bacon, and steak yesterday."

Chapter 17

ADAM DRUMMOND opened the door to his motel room, holding ice over his swelling eye. That goddamn hick Chief. He'd been so fucking solicitous after their set to, insisting that Adam seek medical care and offering to pay for it. He'd even been upfront that if Adam wanted to file a complaint, he could do so. Almost daring him to do it!

He didn't need to resort to those tactics. He'd settle with Kell Farraday. If he couldn't take him out with his fists, a bullet would do just as nicely, but he could wait, do the smart thing and give it a few months, make it look like a hunting accident when he dealt with him. "Yeah, what?" he growled, glaring at the stranger slouching outside.

His visitor had his face turned away from the street, a rakish fedora shielding his features. "I'm Mylar Anderson, and I believe we can help each other," the man announced. "May I come inside?"

"Not unless you can serve me up the local Chief as shredded dog meat," Adam muttered, still in a bad mood.

"I'm afraid that is where your talents come in, Mr. Drummond."

Adam's eyes narrowed. "How'd you know about me?"

"It's a small town. After I heard about the fight at the tavern earlier, I called a friend who works for *The Seattle Times* and then Googled you. I think you being in town is a happy coincidence. May I come in?"

BODY aching like one huge pulsing bruise, stripped down to the robe that Noah had lent him after he'd suggested Kell soak in the hot tub while he made him a late dinner, Kell leaned against the hallway wall, listening—spying, probably, if you split hairs, but he couldn't give a shit. This was about Noah. This was important.

Noah was in the kitchen, using his wok while sharing with Josh an abbreviated story of Adam, about why Noah had chosen to move to Sullivan's Mountain in the first place.

Kell's chest constricted, but he forced himself to let Noah do this. He knew the more people he talked to about it, the better he would heal. But it was so fucking hard to listen to him expose the embarrassment and self-doubt caused by that creep.

There was no doubt in Kell's mind that Noah had done the right thing. His instincts told him that Adam was a wrong guy and he would have hurt Noah badly, maybe even Josh as well, if Noah hadn't moved them away.

NOAH was saying while stirring freshly chopped onions into his sizzling wok, "I dated Adam after your mother died. But I didn't want you to know we were involved at first because I was worried about the...."

"The gay thing. Dad, I told you that doesn't matter to me. Mom, uh, told me before she died that you might date a guy someday."

"Oh." Noah swallowed. Of course, she'd known, but he'd tried to be a good husband and father, putting his family first. He'd believed in fidelity, so as long as she'd lived, he'd never sought out the kind of attention he might have wished for in another life. "Well, it was kind of like that. I missed your Mom and I met Adam. Do you remember how I told you he was just my friend?"

Josh raised an eyebrow. "Yeah. But you were like, so lame about it, as if I wouldn't figure it out. I mean you went to plays and shit with him."

"Plays and shit translate into dating, huh?" Noah observed wryly.

"Why else would you go?" Josh asked.

KELL could imagine Noah blushing at Josh's blunt words, which made him rub a reluctant smile from his lips. God, he didn't just want Noah in his life, he realized. He wanted *Josh* too. Wanted him enough that he hoped Noah would allow him into the family, just a little.

"Adam gave me a bad feeling," Noah finally confessed. "He showed up at our condo sometimes when I was working out of the blue. He called me all the time. At first I was flattered but...." Noah bit his lip. "Well, one night it got a bit much."

Josh was quiet, and Kell figured the kid was probably fighting similar feelings to those Kell had experienced while beating the shit out of Adam. And Kell, by God, couldn't keep out of it any longer; it was time to deal himself in. He limped into the kitchen, favoring his sore ribs, and sat in the kitchen chair. "Sorry, I was listening," he admitted. Then he rubbed his unshaven jaw. "No, damn it, I'm not sorry."

"Kell!" Noah sighed, giving him a look of exasperation, as if he were hopeless. But Kell noticed he didn't seem really pissed.

"I know you don't want me too close, that you don't need anyone, that you have Josh," Kell said, taking the biggest chance of his life. Shit, his hands were shaking when he reached out for the cold, sweating glass of mineral water Noah offered him. "But here's the thing: I want you both."

Noah put down the utensils he was using for the stir-fry—which thank fuck smelled of more than veggies and tofu—and went to Kell. He squeezed his swollen hand.

"I don't know how to be part of a family. I've never had a boyfriend. I'm... a little rough around the edges." Kell cleared his throat. "Just so you know what you're in for if you want me around."

Josh looked at Kell gravely. "Sounds good to me. You look like shit, Chief."

"Call me Kell," Kell offered. Then he looked to Noah. "As long as it's all right with you?" Noah nodded, face soft.

Josh leaned forward. "So can we kill Adam?"

"No," Noah said.

"If he pushes it, I will deal with him," Kell growled, his shoulders relaxing as he felt the tacit approval as Noah absently played with his fingers. Maybe he'd gone from houseguest to boyfriend. He felt wanted here.

Noah scolded primly, "Violence is never the answer."

Josh's eyes filled with cold anger. "I say we rip off his balls and feed them to the ghost."

Kell reached out and pulled Josh close so that both Matthews men were in his protective embrace. "Maybe we can eat our stir-fry first," he joked, trying to deflect Josh's rage. Truth was, this felt fucking good; it wasn't every day he became part of something. "Since your Dad threatened to teach me how to use a wok, I might as well learn how it's supposed to taste when it's not burned."

"In my house, everyone helps out, cooking, cleaning," Noah said.

"All right," Kell agreed. If cleaning up after himself meant living with Noah and Josh, he'd do it. He'd even eat scrambled tofu for breakfast every morning. That had to spell a commitment.

ALEC rubbed Beau's head, looking at Jade with a relieved smile. "So the vet says he'll be okay?"

Jade looked uncomfortable. "Yeah. Look, about you spotting the money to take him to see one. I totally *will* pay you back. I was just short on account I had to get some parts for my jeep."

Alec cocked his head, wanting to put her at ease. "How about you give my SUV a tune up sometime soon and we'll call it even? You're as good as any mechanic in town, and since we're friends, I know you won't lie to me about what it needs."

She smiled at that idea. "Okay. As long as it's not charity."

"How can it be charity to have a hot girl tuning my engine?" Alec cocked a brow.

"Jerk!" But Jade gave him a once over. Oh, yeah, she was thinking about it.

"Just be sure to wear a short leather skirt and no panties and bend over a lot," Alec drawled. "Just like my fantasies." He knew he was dopey from the adrenaline crash of their long day and night up on the canyon wall, saying stupid things and risking angering touchy Jade. Probably now she'd order him from her house, and he couldn't blame her. Shit!

"Would you stop...?" she huffed, crossing her arms and pacing in her doorway. "I'd take your head off but you look like shit. Still got that headache?"

"Yeah." Alec shrugged, deciding to leave before he further embarrassed himself. He had her thinking about him lately, and he'd worked for years just to get to that point.

"Where you goin'?"

"Uh, just back to my SUV. Thought I'd drive to the diner and get something to eat." And then he planned to park his truck outside her house to keep a lookout, not that he was telling his independent Jade about that.

"Nope, stay here with me instead."

Alec blinked. No way she was asking him to—"What did you say?"

"I mean, uh, I'll feed you. And I figure you're so with the Boy Scout shit, you'll sleep out in your truck tonight to protect the little woman if I don't invite you in anyway."

"Jade." Alec's face sobered. "I *saw* the ghost."

"Is he… shit." Jade swallowed. "I think I maybe saw him once too. I told myself he was just passin' through, but once a week I put out cookies and they are always gone the next day. You don't think he's the one who killed Morley, do you?"

Alec rubbed the back of his stiff neck. "No idea, but he was dressed crudely and he had a scabbard for a knife. I hope not, Jade. Because if he did, this town is going to hunt him down."

"I know it," Jade said. "I wish there was something we could do, Alec. Anyway… in the meantime, I got an extra room so you can stay over if you want."

Alec followed her into her house. There was no question. "I want," he told her.

"WHAT I hear is some kind of vengeful ghost is up on the mountain killing people," Adam Drummond shared with his guest while drinking some of the very fine vintage scotch Anderson had offered him. "That's what the guy at the bar told me."

"Ghost," Anderson sighed, examining his hat as he sat on the twin bed opposite the badly bruised Adam. "That silly rumor. I have seen the 'ghost', and I sincerely doubt he poses any threat. But he is useful."

"So nothing's haunting the mountain?" Adam sounded disappointed.

Anderson forced himself not to roll his eyes, reminding himself he needed Adam. He had to take care of things, just like always. "No ghost."

"Oh, bummer. I'd really like to see that bastard Farraday get torn apart by an angry spirit."

"Mr. Drummond, never mind ghosts. Do you want to make some extra money or not? It does involve causing possible trouble for the local chief."

Drummond rubbed his purpling eye. "I want to fry that bastard's balls."

Now they were getting down to business, which Anderson understood. "Very good. I can certainly understand the need to even the score. He took your man, didn't he? I'm also a... possessive man."

"Yeah, okay. What do we do?"

Anderson smiled dryly. "Why, we go hunting, of course. But first, there's something I need you to do."

Chapter 18

NOAH lit the wood fireplace in Kell's guest room. One of the things he'd liked about this house was it came with efficiently designed real wood fireplaces as well as electric ones downstairs. And there were backup systems—there was a generator hut next to the pool, so if they lost power, it could kick in. Despite needing a makeover in a major way, the house was sound.

"Did you ever think it was strange that an entire family ran from this house?" Noah mused.

"Yes, I thought it was strange, so I looked them up. They said they had their reasons," Kell shrugged. "Maybe the fact their relative, Ralph Hindle, had been in some accident on the side of Sullivan's Mountain turned them off."

"So you think they were frightened away?" Noah swallowed and lowered his voice. "That they knew something about what's happening on this mountain?"

Kell sat on the edge of his bed, cupping his knees, his face still colorful from his encounter with Adam, though he held himself with more ease after a long soak in Noah's hot tub. "I don't know, Noah. At the time, no. Now... it's not so cut and dried."

"I'm sure folks in town think something scared them off, like the so-called ghost." Noah put more kindling in, watching as it ignited in bright bursts, thinking that was how he felt whenever he got close to Kell. He recognized that part of the reason for this conversation was easing closer to intimacy with him. His heart was pounding!

"I can't help rumors. I deal in fact." Kell shook his head. "What is a mystery is what happened with Morley Orris, but I think we're getting closer to figuring that one out. And anyway, this house has had a turn of good luck; you and Josh came here and made this place your home."

"We're trying to do that," Noah observed, pensive.

"I think you are." Now Kell got to his feet, and his warm body was a breath apart from Noah's. He put his arms around him from behind as they both stared into the fire. "You certainly stood your ground with Adam."

"So did you!" Noah's lips quirked. "Emphatically."

"Yeah, *ouch.*" Kell leaned his head closer to Noah's. "I'm not a young man anymore. I even find the odd gray hair nowadays."

"It's sexy," Noah said honestly, hiding a smile since Kell had more than the odd gray hair at his temples, but it *was* sexy. "I don't want a young romance for a young man. I want to enjoy every part of falling for the right person."

"I don't remember it being very romantic when I was younger," Kell admitted whimsically. "More like scratching the itch, hot, fast."

"Oh, yes, you've definitely matured," Noah teased.

Kell touched his lips to Noah's, and Noah's heart gave a big thump. "I've learned patience. I don't have to like it, but I have learned that good things do come to he who waits."

Noah moaned when Kell outlined his lips with his warm, sure tongue. His fingers clenched in Noah's shoulders. Oh, Lord! Kell was an experienced, thorough lover. "Am I your good thing?" he rasped.

"NOPE." Kell's eyes warmed at Noah's poorly disguised disappointment. Then, feeling a need to grope toward romance, he continued awkwardly, "I think maybe my last thing. All right?"

"Wow," Noah breathed.

"Wait, 'wow' is scheduled for later on in the evening."

"Is it?"

"Those shy glances you give me make me hard. Fuck, I have it bad. I was supposed to drill you into the mattress, not feel things, other than with my dick."

"Chief, you're positively poetic."

"Damn straight. Is it working?" Kell reached for the wine that Noah had brought up, finding it surprisingly perky with a nice sting. Noah was a hell of a cook, even if he did have strange ideas about tofu. Brownies! Christ! But they had been damned tasty, once Kell stopped thinking they were made of mashed-up bean curd.

"I'll let you know." *Kiss.* "Thanks for being there. Even though you weren't exactly invited," Noah commented drolly.

Kell lifted a shoulder, watching as Noah opened another of his shirt buttons, spreading the material and revealing Kell's bruised and muscled chest. An appreciative and timid hand swept his skin, and Kell wanted to groan. "What do you expect from your caveman?"

"Are you really mine?"

Kell took a deep breath, feeling as if he were parachuting into uncertain territory. He didn't usually trust folks too easily; it was a trait he'd learned as a foster kid, not knowing what one home would be like, another set of adults. He'd buried the need for a family of his own pretty quick and learned to be self-contained. "If you want me."

"Josh and I have indicated we like you around." Noah gave him a clear-eyed look before continuing to touch the vivid flowers of bruising on Kell's chest. "Shit. I hope never to see Adam again. Is it wrong that I was motivated to move because of him?"

"Wrong to want to be happy? I don't see that. You regrouped, you learned to take better care of yourself. But don't worry about seeing him again; you won't. He checked out of his motel."

"You have someone watching him?"

Kell nodded, not making any bones about it. "Hell, yeah. I don't trust him as far as I can throw him. This is my town."

"Anyone tell you that you're a throwback to Wyatt Earp?" Noah's lips curled into a tentative smile, and Kell pulled him into his arms, giving free rein to his possessive side since Noah wasn't objecting.

"I'm asking myself if I'm ready to go further with you," Noah admitted.

"Why not?" Kell was nuzzling Noah's throat. He pushed his cock against Noah's hip so Noah was aware of Kell's desire, but he didn't try anything else.

"Well... Josh."

"Nope. I locked the door while you were busy with placing the wood in the fire." Kell cupped Noah's chin. "Do you mind?"

"No. I'm just getting accustomed to the water, you know?"

"Yes. I'd never want Josh to see us, uh, doing stuff, but he might catch me kissing and hugging you because I'm going to do that." Kell pushed back Noah's curls and gave him a tender kiss. "I have to go see Makepeace soon. He wants to talk to me about something."

"Something that will bring you closer to solving our mystery?" Noah asked hesitantly.

Kell sighed. "Fuck, I hope so. I'm getting tired of folks being scared."

Noah frowned. "I just hope no one else gets hurt before this is resolved."

"I hope to prevent that," Kell said. "Still don't have a fucking clue what Morley Orris was up to, though I gave Makepeace his journal full of business notations for his pot crop. Hopefully he can make sense of the type of short hand used."

"You work so hard," Noah said, leaning against Kell and stroking his arm gently. Kell's shirt hung from his wrists now, baring his upper body like a model for a sculptor. He rather liked the feeling of being shy Noah's sex object.

"Yeah, that's my work, but I like taking care of people." Kell put an arm around Noah, bringing him closer so his dressed body rubbed against Kell's partial nudity. He loved the feel of the smaller man's shirt grazing against his nipples, the two of them slowly sizzling like the vegetables Noah liked to cook in his wok. "What about your work? You don't talk about it much."

"Mmmm, writing about software advancements. It's pretty cut and dried, but it's regular money."

"Makes sense, you being a single parent, that you'd want something reliable," Kell said. "Plus you can live and work anywhere."

"Yep. Also, Josh's mother had money, so…."

"What was she like?" Kell tilted his head, his breath catching in his chest when Noah's finger went to his heavy silver belt, stroking the figure of a half-man, half-wolf.

"Margaret settled for me," Noah said on a sigh. "We got drunk one night in college and made Josh. I think she knew, right away, knew there was a part of me that wasn't fully with her, but we were happy, best friends. It was wrenching when she died."

"I'm sorry." Kell reached out and cupped Noah's cheek. "You made a helluva kid."

Noah leaned forward, eyes holding Kell's, and took his kiss. He was becoming more confident, his hands loosening Kell's belt.

Kell's hand slapped down over Noah's. "Noah," he growled. This was it, his Waterloo. "If you touch my cock, I'm going to come. And I want to come on your skin, on your penis."

Noah's irises were only a thin rim of gray. "Jesus! Kell, what you say…."

"Too much?"

"Honest. Raw."

"Raw is how I want to—" Kell cut himself off. Crazy! He couldn't be saying he wanted that kind of commitment to Noah, taking him without protection. It was too fucking early for that, he knew, even if it had settled in his bones that this thing between them was inevitable. "When I come back after seeing Makepeace, I'd love a back rub," Kell said, giving Noah an out if needed.

Noah swallowed, heart pounding visibly in his throat. His touch, scent, called to Kell. He wanted to mount, to push inside and spill. To conquer what was his. "Just a back rub?"

"Well, no, actually," Kell said calmly. "I thought I'd suck your cock."

Noah flushed, but he didn't say no, and he didn't pull away and run screaming. Kell thought that was progress. That, and Noah had pulled down Kell's zipper now, and Kell's erection fell out, heavy, unsubtle.

"That's all?"

"No, I thought you'd suck mine too," Kell rasped, his eyes heavy lidded as Noah leaned down and licked one of his nipples. He just about yelled. Fuck! Noah's lips, tongue, teeth on him. "Baby, bite down harder on me," he pleaded. "I can take it. I want it!"

"Kell, you're all rainbow colored," Noah remarked, obviously concerned. His hand petted Kell, finding the slender thread of hair, following the path until he grazed Kell's penis.

Kell laughed, pulling Noah close and biting him just under his ear with measured strength. "I want your scratches on my back," he whispered in Noah's ear. Noah's hands clenched into muscle, and then they were kissing, kissing like they were drowning and this was the last taste, the last kiss ever. Teeth clicked, jarred, a little clumsy—

Kell fell back, yanking Noah over him, reaching down, frantic, tearing Noah's sedate slacks open, and then hot, silky skin filled his hand, and then they both filled his hand, and was there anything more satisfying, more gut-wrenching, than two cocks held in his fist? "Rut in my hand. Do it!" Far gone, Noah thrust, his humping a messy collusion against Kell's grip, his breath panting hot against Kell's neck as his dilated eyes held Kell's. Kell reached down and feathered a delicate finger over Noah's balls, hard against his body, sleek, soft skin, warm, so Kell also petted, admired. "God, I want to tie you up! I want to hold you down, crush you into the bed."

"Don't think…" Noah huffed, face tight. "We're going to last. This time."

Kell laughed, but then his laughter cut like a light switch when Noah began to move in earnest, rutting against him as he'd demanded. At the peak moment, he leaned over Kell, mashing Kell's hands against the hardwood floor, covering him with his slighter body, pale skin, blue veins, pink prominent nipples swollen from Kell's touch, taking command of Kell in a way that had never happened before. Kell sure as fuck wouldn't have allowed it with his handcuffs and his macho belt, the tools of his trade, that and all the tricks he bent over who got off on having a cop's cock up their ass.

Captivated, Kell could only watch, and then he gasped when Noah bit his neck, just above the collarbone, marking him, biting him with feeling. Noah taking him made his toes curl and his body arch, and then he was coming on Noah as Noah came on him, tangled together.

Chapter 19

"SEE the scoring on the bone?" Daniel Makepeace pointed out laconically, cracking open some pistachios as he watched Kell look over his findings. "I compared it to the impressions in your raccoon's remains as well as Morley Orris's. It's a match."

Kell folded his arms, thinking that he didn't want to see any more people in his town reduced to what could fill a small plastic box. Something had to be done. Damn. "So you're saying it's a strong possibility that the same killing tool was used in both cases?"

"I can't be absolutely sure of Hindle since his body was eaten by a variety of animals a long time ago, but these victims were fresh, so yes, I'm confident about that much, anyway. See, there was one possibility I hadn't explored when I began my analysis." Daniel bit his lip.

Kell's brows lowered, and he dogged Daniel's heels as the pathologist circled the remains, studying them with his head cocked. "I have a strong feeling I'm not going to like it. First, tell me, what *aren't* you confident about, Daniel?"

"Well, I can't follow all the jargon in Morley's diary, so I've been handicapped in that sense. I won't give you the tired disclaimer of 'damn it, Jim, I'm a pathologist, not a pot grower'."

"You just did," Kell noted sourly, trying to rub the headache from his temples. He'd looked for some aspirin at Noah's house and come up with a suggestion of peppermint oil and a massage. It appeared his new boyfriend was also a homeopath as well as a sometimes-vegetarian. "So what aren't you telling me?"

164

Daniel sighed. "It's the imprint of the killing knife. It troubles me, since near as I can figure out, it's something that might have been manufactured in Africa. The blade shares certain characteristics with something carved by hand there. From the wounds I've examined, I ran a simulation, and I can project that whatever is being used can disembowel someone very efficiently."

Kell's gut tightened in a sympathetic reaction. "Uh huh. But why the hell use that kind of knife? You can pick up less distinctive blades."

"I'd say there would only be two reasons. One, it's the only blade you have, or two, you have a specific purpose in mind in using one, perhaps pointing suspicion in a certain direction."

"Shit." He might have to pick up some Tylenol in his office if Makepeace didn't have any. Noah had told him that pain meant he had to treat the whole person or some shit. He was definitely taking a canister of aspirin up to thei—uh, *Noah's* place.

Daniel pushed back his rumpled hair. "I have a feeling whatever it is we're missing is like pornography," he noted ruefully. "You'll know it when you see it."

"Come on, you've been reading that journal for days now. You must have some ideas."

Daniel didn't look happy. "I know Morley was maybe blackmailing a few people here in town. Too many to narrow down as yet, but there are records of payments made, and some of the initials are familiar."

"What about what Alec described seeing?"

"Alec saw something in the dark and then he fell, so we can't be sure... but a 'wild' boy? It really sounds like science fiction. How could some kid survive up there?"

"Well, keep on it, Daniel, but I don't want you or anyone else going up there into the forest until I'm ready to go hunting. I left a message for Anderson, telling him to leave off looking for his missing gun until I'm sure it's safe up there. *If* that's the reason he was prowling the woods."

Daniel shook his head. "He is an old-time hunter and fisherman. But one thing you should know… I did find trace residue on that raccoon. I think whoever cut it up shot it first."

Kell blinked. "Shot it. Why shoot it and then cut it up with a primitive blade?"

"Like I said, someone may have a reason for pointing in a certain direction to throw us off."

"Hmmm." Kell's brows lowered. "In other words, pointing to our 'wild man'."

WHEN Kell pulled out his keys on his way out, Daniel offered, "I'll keep you apprised of anything else I come up with. And Kell? If and when you go looking for this killer, I want to go with you."

"Forget it," Kell said flatly. "I'm not risking any more people."

"Right. Except yourself."

"That's the plan."

"So have you shared this plan with your new boyfriend?"

Kell flushed. "Uh… say, do you know anything about tofu? Noah likes the shit, and I thought I'd bring some home with me for dinner, but I got no fucking clue what to buy."

Daniel gave a crack of surprised laughter that made Kell turn redder. "*Tofu?* Man, you've got it bad!"

"SOFT tofu." Noah blinked at the packages Kell had put on his purple-stained marble counter. "Chocolate… and strawberry flavored."

"There's some hard in there too. And, uh, extra firm." Kell cocked a wicked brow, smirking in victory. "I thought you could do more with something hard rather than... you know, just soft."

Noah touched the plastic sealed squares before shaking his head at Kell's double meaning. "Extra firm. You're such a tease."

"No, I'm not." Kell's face was suddenly serious. "I never tease. I'll take you all the way, baby, I promise."

Noah gasped as Kell's warm lips nuzzled the back of his neck. Kell's hands curved around his belly and stroked it over his T-shirt, but he appreciated the way the bigger man didn't grope for his sex, considering Josh could walk in on them in the kitchen at anytime.

"Kell." Noah felt years of sexual frustration bubble up. He wanted to ask for more... and he also wanted to ask that they take it easy. He hated that he was so confused sometimes. His body wanted Kell, but the shadow of Adam was still there, like a smudgy impression pressed into his heart. It came and went, whispering for him to be wary about giving himself again.

"It'll be okay," Kell said, as if reading Noah from his stiff body language. "So... what do we put in the wok? I kind of thought the chocolate tofu would be cool."

Noah's hand covered Kell's where it rested on his belly. He was hard and aching, and he could feel Kell's erection prodding him from behind, but he had a meal to prepare, and Kell seemed to understand that. Their passion would simmer while they waited, like their meal.

"Why the sudden enthusiasm for tofu? I figured from the way you acted when you first saw it in my fridge you thought it would make your balls drop off," Noah said ruefully.

"Not at all. I'm really very, uh, new age."

Noah cocked a brow. "Uh huh."

"Okay, maybe more like old world," Kell confessed. "I told you I'm new at this relationship shit. I thought if I tried a little of the things you like and you tried a little steak and eggs...."

Just then, Josh walked into the kitchen, but he didn't look ruffled as he took in Kell snuggling his dad. Instead, he gave Kell an amused look as he took in the variety of tofu on the counter. "You bought dessert?"

"Dessert?" Kell asked blankly.

Josh laughed. "Yeah, that's dessert tofu."

Chapter 20

"WHAT'S the deal? I washed the sheets," Jade said, crossing her arms defensively as she lingered in the guest room doorway, looking at Alec. Well, looking at his ass as he bent over to take off his shoes. And his wide shoulders. And his slim waist. He was shirtless, his skin smooth, and she bet it would be warm to the touch.

"Huh? No, I was lost in thought. Sorry, I just got off the phone with Kell. Just... trying to understand what's happening, what exactly I saw. I think Kell intends to go hunting soon."

Jade walked in the room, brushing a nonchalant hand over the dresser and then the desk. "You going with him, I suppose?"

"Figured, yeah," Alec agreed, turning and fixing his dark velvet gaze on her. "That boy... he looked untamed, but... scared, Jade."

"Then I want to come too. Watch your back. I mean, if he's living wild, there's no saying he didn't kill Morley and carve up that raccoon to frighten folks. But I hope not."

"Jade...." Alec reached out and took her hand, anchoring her to the side of the bed. "I won't get hurt."

"You got hurt already!" She sat down with a huffy sound of disgust. "Some fucking ex-Ranger hero. With all those muscles, I'd've thought you could take better care of yourself." She gave him a scornful glance.

Alec grinned. "You noticed them, huh?"

She rolled her eyes. "Please. You obviously want to look good."

"For someone, yeah." He cupped her cheek. "Thanks for pushing me to take a nap. I am done in, especially from doing paperwork. Kell was worried about my head, so he suggested I could blow off most of it for now, though. I think maybe I can sleep if I have two things…."

"What?" The wary frown was back. He used a thumb to stroke it, as if wanting to erase that emotion and whatever reason she had to carry it.

"A night-light would be good."

"A night-light?" Jade repeated blankly.

"Sure. Have you been able to sleep lately without one? Come on."

Jade found herself laughing, something the fool man made her do. "I guess maybe I have a couple. Do you want Mickie or Minnie?"

"I've always been partial to Minnie, myself," he admitted, smiling at her as she went into the linen closet in his room and dug out a plastic garish-colored night-light.

After Jade stuck it in the wall, switching it on, she asked him, "So what's the other thing you need?" her voice sounded husky to her own ears.

"Would you hold me for a minute, Jade?" He was sitting on the bed now, leaning against the headboard. His eyes were half-closed, making him look sleepy with his rumpled hair.

She slipped onto the bedspread to join him, taking a deep breath. There was an awkward pause before she wrapped her arms around him. "I'm not big on cuddling," she admitted. "Usually, you know, *after,* I leave. I don't invite guys to come here. This is my place."

"So you've never shared this bed with anyone else?" Alec asked, looking pleased.

Jade shook her head. "The guy thing... I never got it right," she said. "So I figured, why bring him here? Maybe I'll be thinking of my mistake every time I walk through my home."

"Smart, but you've been missing out; cuddling's the best part," Alec commented, covering her hands. He closed his eyes, still smiling.

"You're such a woman," she said, smiling back at him now he couldn't see her.

"That's sexist. And, yep."

When she thought he was asleep, she muttered against his neck, "I'll keep you safe, damn you."

NOAH surprised Kell by knocking on his bedroom door as Kell was removing his shirt later. He was used to living alone, but Noah was diffident, courteous, treating Kell as a guest sometimes, like someone who was part of the family others. He decided he liked it. Studying the other man, he raised his eyebrows as he noted Noah had brought a robe, toiletries, and... whoa. Lube and condoms in shy Noah's hands?

"Hey." Kell swallowed, feeling oddly nervous. He couldn't figure it out. He'd intended to fuck Noah from the moment he'd met him. Envisioned it a hundred times, but now... now all he felt was *not ready*. What was wrong with him? He'd had a lot of hot encounters, sweaty body slamming against sweaty body, biting the neck of the man he covered, always pleasing his lover.

But this was Noah.

"I didn't want Josh to... well, for us to have to make trips back and forth between our rooms for, uh, supplies or something. It might be awkward."

Kell frowned. "He can't hear us where he is, right?" There were two rooms between Kell's guest room and Josh's, including a small TV room and Noah's own master bedroom.

Noah shook his head, but color touched his cheeks. "No, but he knows I'm going to sleep here with you tonight."

Oh. Well, Kell hadn't known, and by damn he had to take a deep breath. His hands were shaking, so he put them in his pockets. "Sounds good. He's, uh, okay with it?"

"He told me to trust you."

Kell's head fell forward. "Oh man." He had to close his eyes, afraid of what might be revealed. "Noah, not to kill my macho seducer image but... I'm not ready to use those." He indicated the condom and lube on the blue robe.

"Oh." Noah blinked. "Well, I thought I should be... prepared, just in case."

"Okay." Kell sat on the bed, seeing his reflection in the mirror, tired, unshaven, red-eyed, all rumpled bear. He noticed his jeans were tenting, but he made no effort to hide that. Noah had to know how much he wanted him.

THIS new sober side to his aggressive pursuer took Noah aback for a moment, but then he realized he liked it. It felt like this wasn't just him being chased by his caveman anymore. It felt like... a relationship.

He grinned at the idea of calling it that to Kell. Way to freak out his man!

"What?"

"Nothing." Noah's eyes were heavy-lidded as he came around the bed and put his hands on Kell's shirt, helping him unbutton the rest, revealing muscles, smooth skin.... Noah couldn't stop himself from bending closer and taking one of Kell's coppery nipples into his mouth, sucking it hard. Kell gasped, head falling back, hands clenched into fists as if he were fighting to keep from grabbing Noah. "Let's get you undressed."

"WHAT are you thinking about?" Jade asked in a sleepy voice. She'd been holding him for over an hour, and Alec was drifting, just enjoying her firm body close to his own, her arms looped around him, giving off capable Jade-comfort.

"Remembering a night we met up when I was just a kid," he confessed. "I knew you were the one, Jade."

Jade groaned. "Alec."

"Hey, don't you remember?"

Jade's brows rose. "I seem to remember this annoying kid hanging around and attempting to come to my rescue."

Alec smiled. "You do remember." He closed his eyes, seeing it again, satisfied because right now she was right where he'd dreamed she would be. With him.

"You can't treat me like that! I want to go for a walk, I'm going!" Jade Moreton cursed her boyfriend. Boyfriend du jour, fifteen-year-old Alec thought bitterly, eavesdropping.

A moment ago, the couple had been moaning. Plastered against Jade's hot little jeep parked directly behind him. Kissing and feeling each other up and making Alec stiffen in his pants as he watched them guiltily. He hadn't set out to spy; he was just sitting in his Dad's car, waiting to pull out when they showed up and started making out behind him.

Just Jade and another of her guys.

He wanted her to see him, Alec, but he knew he was just a kid to her.

"Slut!"

Jade shoved her boyfriend. In his rearview mirror, Alec saw the big man raise his hand to hit Jade, so he flung open the door to his own vehicle and strode over to the surprised couple, clearing his throat and staring into the eyes of the twenty-something guy. Shit. He was big. "Don't hit her. Just don't do that."

"Fuck off, kid."

Alec crossed his arms and leaned against the car next to Jade. "You fuck off," he said.

When the boyfriend looked like he was going to make something of it, Jade intervened. "Jesus, just take off and leave the kid alone, you jerk!"

A COUPLE of minutes later, Jade's head fell back. "Well, fuck. No sex for me tonight and damn, the making out got me, uh, never mind," she muttered, as if becoming aware of who she was talking to. "Thanks, kid."

Alec swallowed and then nodded. "There are a lot of things you could do to, um, pleasure yourself. Toys. No penis needed."

Jade's eyes widened. "Aren't you the knowledgeable one."

"I've studied sex," Alec admitted, shrugging in embarrassment. "I fell for a girl so I decided I should understand her body."

"Wow... lucky girl," Jade said, and she seemed sincere. "Be sure to look me up in a few years if she doesn't latch onto you."

Alec's throat tightened. He burned to tell her, but he knew it was too soon. Knew there was no way she'd take him seriously. "Yeah," he rasped. "I'll do that."

Jade stared at him for a long moment, and he could feel his heart beating in his ears and his gut locked with yearning for her. She gave a little shrug and opened her jeep door. "Thanks again, uh. I don't even know your name."

Alec held her eyes. "You will."

"I ALWAYS wanted to ask you back then how you would have suggested I get off—but you were too young," Jade mused, a small smile playing over her lips. "You were a Boy Scout even then, helping me out."

Alec gave her an amused look. "I'm a big boy now, Jade."

Jade didn't touch that one. Too obvious. Besides, he'd only want to show her, and something told her he didn't need to brag. "So if you were me, how would you get off?" Jade asked bluntly.

ALEC grinned a little. That was his Jade, to the point about her pleasure. They'd been moving toward this moment for days, so he was going to enjoy it. Enjoy her being his, not that she knew she was *his* exactly, but he was working on it.

"I'd use a toy, something that felt good. It's all about texture…."

Jade squirmed. "Uh, yeah, texture. But you only bought your shaving kit."

"So I guess I'd have to improvise. Do you have a washcloth, something… really soft that you use for company? And some runny hand lotion."

Jade blinked, and Alec could see the pulse pounding in her neck. She licked her lips. "Now?"

"You want to get off and I want to get you off," he offered easily.

"Okay." She looked at him. "You know, it's kind of sexy, you being my younger man."

Alec closed his eyes when she got up so she wouldn't see what being called *hers* at last did to him.

JADE returned with a bottle of hand lotion and an Egyptian cotton washcloth, hesitating a moment, dark eyes wide, before handing them to Alec.

"Take your hair out of that ponytail?" he asked, wanting to see it.

Wordlessly, she slipped it free, tawny brown hair falling around her face.

He patted the bed, and she sat close to him, reaching out to put a hand on his knee.

Alec took the cream, removed the lid, and poured some onto the washcloth.

"What will you use that for?"

"I could show you." Alec's voice was guttural. *Jade.*

Jade shifted, eyes on the towel. "You seem so sweet. I stayed away from you because I didn't want to hurt you, Alec."

"I don't need you to protect me, Jade. Not by staying away," Alec chided. Then he smiled, pretending confidence he didn't quite feel since this was her, his dream woman.

Jade reached out and clicked off the bedside lamp, leaving them in the soft glow of the Minnie night-light.

"OKAY, um, you have to lift your skirt and take off your panties," Alec ordered, glad it was dark so Jade couldn't see him blush. He didn't want to blow his macho image.

Jade lifted her short pink leather skirt, and Alec saw she wasn't wearing any underwear. She must have removed it in the bathroom. Whoa. He broke out in a sweat, seeing her.

She spread herself, her depths pink and glistening like the inside of ripe fruit. Alec stared. He couldn't help it. She was… oh, man….

"You look at me like you've never seen a girl before." She was playing with her nipples through her T-shirt now, her natural directness coming out, her long, lush hair tangled over her chest.

"*Stop!*" Alec smacked her hand, making her eyes widen in shock. "Do as I tell you. It'll be better."

"Hey!"

"Do you want to feel good or not?"

Jade bit her lip. "I don't take orders. Um, except at the diner."

"I'm going to give you mind-blowing pleasure, unless you don't like the idea?" Alec cocked a brow.

"Bossy!"

"Pot, kettle," Alec mocked, pouring more oil into his hands and warming it by rubbing it briskly. Holding her gaze, he let it drip onto her open body.

Jade hissed and thrust her hips up, obviously liking the sensation. Her nipples pebbled through the cotton of her shirt.

"Put your hands above your head and keep them there," Alec coaxed softly.

After a pause, Jade obeyed. She looked like a wanton goddess, legs spread, eyes heavy-lidded, body open and partially revealed. When Alec touched her with the washcloth, she gasped. "*Harder,*" she prodded.

"*No.* I'm in control, Jade, and I want to take it easy with you." Alec could smell her excitement, and his penis ached for her, but he could put off his own relief. What he wanted now, after all these years, was to bring her to climax. He wanted her to come for him the way she'd never come for all the men she'd had.

He stroked her obliquely, glancing, gentle caresses that he knew couldn't satisfy. He'd learned to do this kind of thing by experimenting on himself, touching himself for hours until he finally allowed himself to come.

"*Oh*...." Jade spread wider, her hands gripping the headboard as Alec attended to her needs. "I can't... I need it harder!"

"I told you 'no'. Just lie there like a good girl."

"You're kind of pissing me off."

177

"And turning you on."

After he'd stroked her for what seemed like hours, Jade was bathed in sweat. She lifted her T-shirt, revealing her bare breasts. When she went to touch her nipples, Alec pushed her hand away with his free one. He pinched one nipple and then other as her body glowed and writhed, alive now under his touch. "You'll come from me doing that. Touching your breasts," Alec told her.

"Umm."

He pinched her nipples harder as she twisted against the washcloth between her legs, her body so stimulated now that he knew she was close.

"You're beautiful, Jade," he whispered and then pinched one of her nipples—*hard.*

Jade climaxed, her hands clawing the sheet and then his arm where he was seeing to her.

"OH, MY...." She blinked at him after, eyes doe-brown, soft. "That was...."

"You're the most beautiful woman I've ever seen," Alec said, tossing aside the washcloth. He righted her clothing and then gathered her carefully in his arms. "Go to sleep, sweetheart," he said.

Chapter 21

BEMUSED, Kell sat on the bed and watched as Noah untied his boots and removed them, followed by unrolling his socks. Noah took his time, holding Kell's gaze, the moment simmering between them. Anticipation, mature awareness. They weren't kids, either of them. It made Kell want Noah all the more because he respected him.

Next, Noah removed Kell's partially unbuttoned plaid shirt, his eyes skimming shyly over the muscle on Kell's chest and shoulders—making Kell feel damn glad he spent so much time groaning while lifting weights or huffing through sit-ups.

Finally, Noah reached for Kell's belt buckle, fingering the distinctive silver piece. "I am fond of this belt buckle."

Kell chuckled. "You've wanted to do that since I met you."

"In your dreams," Noah said, rolling his eyes at Kell's preening. "I finally figured out that it's a man and his spirit animal."

Kell smirked. "Alec told you he bought it for me one Christmas."

"Yes." Noah looked at Kell. "It's nice, you two being such good friends."

"I never thought of him any other way, especially since he's so fixed on Jade," Kell said, wanting to stamp out any insecurity Noah might have.

"I guessed that already, but it's nice to hear it, Kell. Thank you," Noah said softly.

He soon had Kell's jeans off and then his underwear peeled down, revealing the unsubtle erection that prodded the air between them.

"Do you like what you see?" Kell asked, wanting to hear it—okay, maybe wanting a touch of reassurance himself.

"I didn't want to like you at all, but I do," Noah confessed, lifting up on his toes to kiss Kell, cupping his cheek.

Kell felt a sudden misgiving shift under his breastbone. "I have to go into the woods to continue my investigation soon, Noah," he whispered. "I have no idea what is going on, but I have to make my town safe somehow. I have to make you and Josh safe."

Noah frowned. "Can't you get someone else to do it?"

Kell shook his head, sighing. "I did make a couple of calls, but at best, I'd be looking at help a month from now. Plus it turns out the land surrounding Sullivan's Mountain is a reserve, which further complicates things."

"But you're still planning on investigating."

"I don't want to," Kell admitted ruefully. "I know you don't like it."

"Because I care about you. I don't want my safety at the price of losing you."

"Hey!" Kell leaned his forehead against Noah's. Tenderness. He guessed he was getting better at showing it.

Noah opened his mouth to argue further, and Kell kissed him, pulling the other man down on his lap. He nuzzled Noah's neck, liking the smell of the pool still there, probably from the laps Noah did every night. He had that slim swimmer's build that Kell found so hot. "I want you to know this was supposed to be a quick bang, only it's not."

"You romantic!" Noah wrapped his arms around Kell, as if getting caught up in the spirit of their moment. Kell didn't think he was finished arguing with him, but right now…. "I wish you wouldn't go out there again."

"Nothing will happen, baby. I promise I'll come back to you; hey, it's a small town with very little going on most of the time, other than Moss acting up in the road house." Kell kissed Noah again, lifting his T-shirt from his body, and, while Noah's arms were still raised, running a finger down his arm through the tuft of dull blond hair there. Noah shivered.

"I never imagined," he mused.

"Oh, yeah," Kell agreed.

AT LAST the men curled on the guest bed, Noah lying on top of Kell, eyes tightly closed as Kell stroked his back. "I'm pretty nervous."

"Well, you haven't had wildly good experiences with gay sex."

"So what do we do about it?"

Kell warmed at the "we," playing with Noah's fingers. He was enjoying the anticipation, like lightning jumping just under the skin. "I thought we'd try some old-fashioned sixty-nine."

"I haven't sucked anyone off before," Noah admitted. "For a while after my mistake with Adam, I wouldn't even look at pictures I used to find arousing on web sites."

"You don't have to now. You can just give me a hand job, you know, if you want. Are you willing to experiment?"

Pupils dilated so only a thin rim of gray surrounded them, Noah nodded. But Noah laughed when they shifted around on the bed to face the sex of their partner, as if catching that there was something playful about it, just moving into position. *I am going to suck you off. You are going to suck me off. This is so not serious.*

Kell didn't move for the goodies first. Instead, he stroked Noah's hip in slow circles, feeling the residue of tension still there. "Shh. Just relax. You'll like it."

Noah shrugged. "I keep thinking, who goes first?"

"Don't worry about being polite. Just let me touch you." Kell gently cupped Noah's balls and nuzzled him with his open mouth, fingernails scraping gently on the sensitive skin between Noah's sac and cock. He licked Noah and then puffed his breath over where he'd touched.

Noah hissed at the ghost sensations, his hips jerking. "Oh!" His eyes blinked in surprise. Oh, yeah, that had zapped him awake in the best way possible.

"Stay absolutely *still.* Can you do that?" Kell commanded.

"Uh."

"And, if you're a good boy, I'll suck your cock."

NOAH'S penis flexed in response to Kell's words. The idea that he had to hold still and give himself to Kell, trust him, was both hard and arousing. "Please."

"Do you want to come in my mouth?"

Noah closed his eyes, hissing out a breath as Kell dabbled with fingers and tongue, exploring him thoroughly. He felt intensely sexy and appreciated, as well as nervous. Could he let go of his fears and surrender completely to Kell? "So much," Noah finally admitted.

Kell began to taste and lick Noah. He pried him open so his lips could nuzzle behind his balls before kissing a trail gently up his inner thighs.

Noah shuddered, heart beating in his ears. Since he'd promised not to move, every sensation seemed magnified. He was a prisoner of the sensations Kell built like a bonfire in his body. One hand reached up and gently jerked him once, tugging words, feelings, *sex,* so that Noah wanted to spill. It was so intense, and yet at the same time, he savored his willing helplessness, loving being the concubine, the slave that Kell had told him once he'd fantasized seeing Noah play.

Kell's touch was both delicate and raspy, his hands careful, but his calluses rousing Noah as he rubbed the sensitive island on Noah's shaft where the wrinkled flesh gathered. "Love how you smell, taste, *feel*," Kell praised, nuzzling Noah. "There's nothing like a man's cock in your mouth, spilling on your skin. I never feel more a man than when I'm sucking cock."

Noah laughed breathlessly. "Believe me, I'm a very happy recipient."

"You are. You're... what did you call my men once? A floozy in my arms. I like that, Noah."

Noah shuddered as Kell gently sucked his cockhead and then took his penis, all of it, accepting him, playing a role that Noah had been convinced he'd never accept at first glance, the giver of pleasure, not the taker.

"You're so fucking gorgeous, baby." Kell petted him soothingly. "You're doing so well. Holding still so your man can see to you."

Noah's balls tightened at the words "your man." Lover, partner, man, master. Kell could be all of them.

"So hard to keep still, I know, but look what a good boy you are," Kell continued to praise as he played with Noah's needy sex. When Kell's teeth bit gently along his crown, Noah gasped, never having experienced the sting of controlled pain.

"It just... it feels so good. I'm sorry." Noah was shaking, feeling like he was shedding an old skin and the new one was so easily bruised.

"Don't be sorry, just give yourself to me. I'll keep you safe." Solemn brown eyes made a vow, and then Noah was sheathed in Kell's mouth.

"Please, Kell! I need to...! Oh, God, please, please, *suck me!*" Noah's hands scrabbled on the sheets as he fought to keep still. He thrust in Kell's mouth, and warm, tormenting velvet pulled back, eluding him, eluding his need to come, oh, God, to come and spill in and on Kell.

He took a deep breath and tried again to keep still while his body quivered like a guitar string played by a master. He was rewarded with a tongue caressing the sensitive skin of his slit. He was riding the edge of coming!

Kell rubbed the small of his back tenderly. "You're being so good, baby, letting me tease you." He took Noah's cock in his mouth again, and Noah moaned, his fingers stretching out, his toes curling, his nipples hard, all his focus on his penis. So close, so close, so close—

Kell gently squeezed Noah's balls, and just like that, Noah couldn't hold back. He sobbed out a breath as his semen spilled easily in Kell's mouth.

"YOU snore," Jade noted. "And it's not adorable."

"You're thinking so loud it woke me up," Alec rasped. He sat up, and she looked at soft skin, tanned on his forearms, pale where he wore his shirt. Muscles defined each patch of territory. She touched him, and he made a purring sound.

"Wow, you purr when I do that?"

"Oh, yeah, when it's you touching me. I mean, I've been thinking about that since I could get hard."

"So I was your pinup girl?"

Alec rolled over so he was partially lying on top of Jade. She didn't pull away or slug him. Her face was curious and receptive. He figured things were looking up.

"Let's kiss," he whispered.

Her lips were warm, and when he wooed her mouth gently, she grabbed his forearms to try to pull him fully on top of her. Alec resisted. "There is no hurry, Jade, so don't push it. Hasn't anyone ever taught you it's better if you wait?"

"I thought we'd get to the good part," she said, squirming. "Waiting is for airport lobbies, or your coffee to percolate in the morning. When it comes to sex...."

He was amused. "You mean you want to get off again?"

"What of it?" Her prickles were back, making him want to both smooth them and raise them.

Alec pulled her over him and resumed kissing her. She softened, and he reached down to the seam of the jeans she'd put on after their first play to walk her dog in the safety of her yard, cupping it in his palm and rubbing against her.

"Oh...." She collapsed against him like a heavy rose resting against the earth. "Not bad."

"Spread a little wider," he encouraged. He unzipped the jeans, his hand slipping inside her panties to stroke her slickness. She hung over him, staring into his eyes as he plied her.

"Confident, slightly rough at the fingertips," she described in a rough voice. "*Heaven!*"

"That's it, sugar. Ride my hand."

WHEN Noah nuzzled Kell's sex, Kell couldn't keep a needy gasp from his lips. Dark eyelashes fluttered shut. He thrust bluntly toward Noah's lips, unable to stop himself, even knowing Noah had never sucked a man before. Shit!

"Fuck!" He was cranky, since he really wanted one of the nice little cocksuckers he knew a few towns over to do him. Kneeling in the gravel outside a club, a young man on his knees.

But no, he didn't. He wanted Noah to be his little cocksucker, not that he figured it was a bright idea to share that description with his vegetarian homeopath politically correct boyfriend. He would probably say Kell was being impossibly retro.

"Didn't you just say 'give yourself to me'?" Noah asked softly. "I haven't done this before, so let me know if…." He cleared his throat. "If you like how I do it."

Kell's hand lost itself in Noah's curls as Noah suckled Kell's big sex. Fuck! It was impossibly satisfying watching Noah's lips part to take him down his throat so that he grazed Kell's pubic hair. Noah's hands cupped his balls, mimicking what Kell had done for Noah, gently squeezing.

"I like that! Noah! Suck it deep, oh, baby, *please*—"

NOAH struggled to accommodate Kell's shallow, ragged thrusts. The tempo and the sweat gleaming on Kell's skin told him that Kell was riding the edge of his control.

Shyly, he licked up and down the stem, swirling his tongue in Kell's slit and feeling the larger man shudder.

"Oh, shit, you're the sweetest little cocksucker, Noah," Kell praised.

Noah's eyes widened. That was so not PC! But so Kell. He nipped Kell's cock head in punishment.

THE touch of pain lancing through him along with the intense lash of pleasure was too much for Kell's strained control. He felt his balls draw up.

"Noah, I'm going to—" Kell twitched to pull away, not wanting to frighten or push Noah too soon. But, God, he wanted to shoot on Noah's face. In his mouth.

Noah grasped his hips and swallowed Kell's cock, and it was too much—

With a lusty cry, tangled under Noah's touch like seaweed, Kell spent in his mouth.

Dazed, he watched Noah lick his swollen lips in the aftermath. He knew it was the caveman part of him, but he couldn't deny to himself he was glad Noah had been brave enough to swallow his come.

He couldn't wait to spatter his mark on him again.

NOAH closed his eyes tightly as Kell snuggled him after their play. "Josh was right."

"About?" Kell frowned, studying Noah's flushed face and tenderly pushing back the hair sticking to his damp forehead. They'd both need a swim to cool off. And maybe a cold beer, if Noah kept something that wasn't fucking organic and went down like mildewed grass.

"About trusting you," Noah whispered softly. "I love you, Kell."

Chapter 22

JOSH woke in a cold sweat, his chest still tight, hurting. He felt an elusive sense of familiarity for the pain he was feeling. Maybe… because his Dad was falling for someone else? Josh was doing his best not to behave like a dork, but he was a little apprehensive of the uncertain waters.

He wiped tears from his eyes and got up from the bed.

He stared out at the woods from his bedroom window, and then, as if it were inevitable, the thing he'd been waiting for since they'd first moved in happened: a figure moved free of the trees and stared up at his window.

Josh frowned, and all the pieces seemed to fall into place, mostly. He had to do something.

"YOU love me?" Kell said blankly. Shit! Was he supposed to say something? He couldn't imagine saying… *that.* He'd never said those words to anyone. A slap on Alec's shoulder said it all. But this?

Sweating, he pulled the bedspread over himself, feeling a sudden need to cover his body. "Um."

"You're scared." Noah grinned. He lay like a nude offering on the bed, his body relaxed and his penis reddened and soft now from their play. Saying those words had obviously not put the fear of God into him.

"Scared? No! No, I, uh. That's nice."

Noah poked Kell, gray eyes leveling on him like the barrel of a Magnum. "*Nice?* Nice is going for a walk. Eating a good meal. But I don't think it covers it when someone you slept with declares himself."

"But we haven't slept together yet. Technically," Kell offered weakly. He reached over and snapped off the light, deciding to avoid this conversation. Noah had just blown out the better part of his brains through his cock. He told himself he'd be up to it... later. Jesus! Way to give him a soft-on.

Love? He'd rather reach under a granite overhang and find a nest of rattlesnakes than take this on. At least he knew what to expect from snakes.

And what if he let himself... care for Noah, and he decided Kell was too rustic for him? They were so different, city class and country denim.

Yet in the darkness, he felt comfortable pulling Noah back into his arms, as if their bodies did not lie. The other man didn't stiffen up or growl at him, which Kell half-dreaded. He was pliant, satisfied. Okay, then. "So let's sleep together now."

JOSH squelched the guilt he felt as he listened briefly at Kell's guest door. Hearing Kell's voice, he decided he should leave *now* while the two men were focused on each other and not him.

He was afraid that if he waited until morning, either his Dad or the Chief might stop him.

A LITTLE while later, Kell woke to find Noah had left the guest bed. He got up, frowning, and only remembered to snag some pajama bottoms at the last moment because he didn't want Josh to see him stalking his father in the nude. And it would be stalking, he grumbled to himself. He didn't have a clue how to respond to Noah's words, but he wanted to be within touching distance. He wanted to wrap his arms around Noah and lean his head on his shoulder and breathe in his scent.

Then maybe he could get some fucking sleep!

He peered into the darkened study and then Noah's bedroom on the upper floor, pausing when he saw Noah, also wearing silk pajama bottoms, leaning against one column of an elaborate cherry four-poster bed carved with cupids and columns and other shit that wasn't anything like what Kell would have chosen for himself. But it had one thing going for it, anyway, which he immediately pictured.

"Nice bed." He imagined silk scarves to tie Noah down using the columns but decided it might be too early to make a comment about that. But the picture of Noah all helpless while he slow-fucked him made his penis stiffen with fresh interest.

He went to the slight man and pulled him into his arms, Noah's back to his front, seating them both on Noah's bed. His throat tightened, and he wished he could give Noah what he wanted, but....

"Needed to run?"

Noah nodded. "I was fine until I woke up and realized that for the first time since my wife's death, I was... sleeping with someone. I'd had sex with someone. But... I guess you do this all the time." Noah shrugged awkwardly. "I guess it wasn't a big deal, what we did."

Kell kissed the back of Noah's neck where the hair curled against his skin. Yeah, warmth, sleek muscles, Noah felt good. Kell's suddenly full erection prodded Noah's backside with enthusiasm. "I told you I don't do sleepovers. I fuck and then I walk."

Noah turned around on Kell's lap, grave gray eyes weighing Kell. It frustrated him, seeing Noah unhappy already. Didn't he just know he'd fuck this up somehow? "So what does that mean?"

"I don't know if I can love someone, Noah, or that I believe in it. I do believe in being honest and in grinding together, needing that moment. I want to see you sweaty under my hands. Want to tie you up." Kell decided he might as well give Noah the rawer side of his want. Noah hadn't run yet. "And I want you to sleep with me every night. I like your skin. I like your muscles and your cock and your scent. I want you close by."

Noah flushed. "I've never been tied up. I'm not sure I can picture that."

"I sure as fuck can!" Kell leaned close and kissed Noah. Deep, hungry, so he groaned when he pulled away. Did they have to keep fucking talking, or could they...?

"Caveman."

Kell smiled. He guessed. "Yeah. Listen." Kell wracked his brain. He couldn't give Noah words he wasn't sure were real. But was there something...? "I think that your first time...." Noah tensed a little, and Kell growled out the rest of his thought, "I think you should do me."

"*WHAT?*" Noah stared into Kell's dark, heated eyes. Eyes full of recent satisfaction and the simmering need for more. He felt nerves knot in his belly. This man wanted him. This man would take him. Penetrate him. He'd even baldly admitted to wanting to tie Noah up. Noah looked at the canopy bed they were sitting on and saw it through Kell's eyes. Trust his caveman to ignore the beautifully carved wood and focus on one aspect his bed might offer.

And now he was suggesting...?

Blank, Noah asked, "Have you ever... been on the receiving end?"

"*No,*" Kell said in a low, intimate tone. One that Noah decided he liked hearing from his lover. His fingers were gentle as they combed through the waves of Noah's hair. "Don't want to now, but if it would make you less apprehensive, I'll let you. Well, maybe once, anyway."

Noah laughed softly. "Now that's enthusiasm!" He swung legs flexible from yoga, martial arts, and swimming so they curled around Kell's hips. Kell's eyes flared, and he reached to pull down the silk that hid Noah's sex, groping for Noah with a sure, confident hand.

Noah felt sweat break out on his forehead and upper lip. He liked that Kell was this way with him. He might even like to be tied down, in more ways than one. "I'll let you tie me up sometime if you let me do it to you."

Kell blinked. "Uh."

"Seems fair."

Kell's eyes narrowed speculatively. "You riding my cock while my wrists are chained to the bed. All right."

"Oh, so I still bottom even when I tie you up?" Noah poked Kell.

"Yep."

Noah leaned against Kell, liking that the other man put an arm around him automatically, finger tracing the sculpted definition that Noah had worked hard to build. "You say you don't know how to love, but the way you take care of me and Josh, I know that we matter to you. It's why I let you close."

"You're not a one-night stand," Kell agreed, stroking Noah's penis absently like a pet he was fond of so that it hardened proudly under his touch. "I'm sorry. Not good with words."

"Man of action," Noah said, bending close to nibble shyly on Kell's earlobe. Kell's hand on him felt so good. He knew he'd come, and he knew that Kell would bring him there, but the lazy touches told him that his lover was in no hurry this time, that this time would be slow and sweaty. "I think I'd rather be with someone who showed me by his actions that he loves me than gave me empty flattery."

"I don't know about that love stuff," Kell admitted, but he wasted no time in shifting so that Noah fell on his back on the bed. He stared into his eyes with deliberate intention before getting to his feet and quietly locking the door.

Then, standing there, tall, whiskered, heavy-eyed, he peeled back his own pajama bottoms, knelt on the bed, and leaned over Noah so their two cocks touched. Noah hissed as Kell fisted them both together, jerking them in a slow, easy rhythm that made Noah raise his legs.

"Put your hands on the headboard, slave boy," Kell whispered. "I'm going to come all over you, and you're going to let me."

JADE blinked awake on her guest room bed, staring at the ceiling blankly for a moment before fragments of what she'd shared with Alec came back to her in little bubbles of heat. Ummm.

"Ride my hand!"

Jesus, who knew the Boy Scout could be so hot? He'd taken her over, given her orders that from any other man would have resulted in a fight, not sex. And she'd gone along with it.

She sat up and saw him standing by the window. He was frowning and looking toward the woods, and she felt his worry. His protectiveness. Like Kell, he was a natural guardian, a natural warrior. And it wasn't exactly PC, but she guessed she liked that. She liked his muscles and his macho side… and his gentleness. Plus, turned out he could actually make her laugh when she didn't want to break a dish over his head.

While she'd been sleeping off the intense encounter, he'd been watching over her.

Butt naked.

Mmm. She eyed the hard, high curves of his ass, picturing her fingers digging in when he fucked her. She wanted it slamming hard, clawing his back. She wanted his eyes holding hers while he covered her.

"Alec," she called softly.

He turned around, and she saw his sex for the first time. He held her gaze, and she had a moment of knowing he wanted her to see him as a man. *Her man.*

"I'm going to fuck your pussy and your mouth and your ass. I'm going to push you against the wall in the alley behind the diner and fuck you there on one of your breaks," he vowed quietly, his eyes burning. "I've wanted you for years, and you can't hide from me any longer, Jade."

NOAH wrapped his hands around the spokes of his headboard, holding Kell's gaze. Kell palmed his cock, hanging over him, breath warm on his face as he worked him, as he worked them both.

"All the time I was a married man, a faithful man," Noah whispered, his body pushing up, closer to Kell, to his care, to his large, masculine hand.

"All the time I was in the army, locking down that part of myself…" Kell murmured, making the parallel. "This is our time, Noah. Look at me. Look into my eyes when you shoot."

"Kell…." A strangled sound. Noah felt that combination of inevitability and helplessness as he gave himself, come spilling, feeling it as it struck his skin from Kell, who held his penis very deliberately, pointed toward Noah's face.

Noah sat up, shaking his head, wiping a hand on the corner of his lips, over his chin.

"I hear it's good for the skin." Kell said.

"YOU'VE hunted wild animals before, yes?" Anderson prodded Adam where he'd set up camp in the woods above the canyon. "If that bloody Chief can't find the boy, then we will, and once we do, there will be no doubt who killed Morley Orris. The people of this town will be very relieved the threat has been taken care of and they can sleep through the night."

Adam picked up spent shells scattered under the trees. He'd been tuning up, readying himself. Imagining Kell Farraday as his target had been fucking satisfying. "Whatever. It's too bad they don't let you go out and shoot big game like in the old days, all that shit about endangered species. Think this'll be like that, hunting for someone for real?"

"Likely. For the moment though, I want you to keep an eye on that Chief you're so fond of, Kell Farraday."

Adam smiled, noting, "Easy enough, since the fucker is staying with Noah. So I'll watch the place, see if an opportunity presents itself." He didn't mention what kind of opportunity. Frankly, he didn't give a fuck what Anderson's deal was. He reached for his gun and his knapsack.

Chapter 23

"HEY," Kell rasped, pulling Noah on top of him, pushing his hair back. He couldn't believe they were together at last.

"I…." Noah shook his head at the unsettled feeling. He wasn't sure why he was experiencing it, so he pushed it aside. "What time is it?"

"Early. Very." Kell snapped on the bedside light, and his face was calm as he studied Noah, the kind of calm that came from confidence. Noah leaned his head against Kell's shoulder. "I don't want any more mystery. I just want my fresh start, my new man." Noah sat back. "New man. Has a nice ring," he said softly.

Kell cupped his cheek. "Anything your new man can do for you, Noah?"

"Yeah." Noah swallowed. "Can we…?"

Kell's eyes widened, and he sat up, pushing his bed hair from his eyes. "I thought you needed me to—fuck, I don't know."

Noah shook his head. "Don't you see, Kell? That you made the offer was enough. You're *not* him. There is just no way I'd ever think that."

"You're not apprehensive?" Kell was stroking Noah's hair as if gentling a frightened animal.

"You'll keep me safe," he said. "Isn't that what you manly tops do?"

Kell gasped out a laugh. *"Manly top?* Have you been watching some of those DVDs I lent you, by any chance?"

"Maybe." Noah smiled. "It did help put me in the right frame of mind, I admit, though I'm not sure at my age I'm that flexible."

Kell swallowed thickly, and Noah felt a rush of tenderness. His *manly top* was clearly as nervous as he was. "You look plenty flexible to me, sugar. From what I've seen of you in the pool and when you've done your Tai Chi shit."

"There's lube and condoms in the drawer in this room too," Noah noted, nodding to his bedside table. Kell's eyes widened. "What, I can't be prepared? I knew this would happen. More than that, the last few days I've wanted it to happen."

"Me too," Kell agreed. He opened the drawer and took out the lube. Then he bent close and kissed Noah. "Oh, you will be prepared, don't worry."

"I'm not."

"Noah, I can't promise this is going to be painless. The first time you take cock—"

"And you'd know a lot about that, right?" Noah teased as a cover. Whenever he held Kell's solemn dark eyes, he felt like he was jumping straight into deep water. Losing himself. "Have you ever been with a... does the term 'almost-virgin' mean the same thing between gay men?"

Kell nodded. "It does and the answer is *no.* I always selected experienced partners."

"Don't you mean *players?"*

"Have it your way, bossy bottom." Kell was warming a large dollop of lube in his palms. "You're clearly a backseat driver." He pushed Noah's legs up, bending him almost in half. "Remind me not to diss that yoga shit you do anymore," he noted as a thick finger found and gently rubbed against Noah's dimple.

AT THE last second before penetration, Noah tensed.

"Hey." Kell hesitated, broaching Noah, sweat running down his sides and into his eyes as he held himself back. He wanted to fuck Noah into the mattress, had wanted it since he'd met him, but now he couldn't, not unless—

"I know you can't…." Noah dropped his gaze. "Can't say you love me. I'm hoping that's a 'yet' thing, and you know, that someday…."

"Baby, we can stop. I can jerk you off." Kell thought it would kill him, but taking Noah without Noah being with him, all the way, felt like shrapnel to the chest.

"I just need to hear it, okay? That you do feel something for me. That this is more than…."

Kell closed his eyes. Noah was pushing him to give up more of himself. He wasn't sure he could say the right thing. "Do you want to know why I don't do relationships?" Kell leaned down and kissed Noah, trying to get him to relax.

"Because you don't want to be tied down, I guess."

"No," Kell said. "Because as a Ranger, I only went places I was prepared for, that I understood. The unknown… it's not acceptable."

"It is scary," Noah agreed, reading between Kell's lines.

Kell leaned his forehead against Noah's. "Let me make love to you now, Noah."

"Why?"

"Because sometimes you scare me." Kell let another chunk of himself go. "All right?"

Noah relaxed, smiling a little now. "I knew it!" Kell lifted a brow and thrust gently, knocking at Noah's door, asking…. Noah's grin softened, and his eyes closed. Kell watched sharply as he made the adjustment, easing his way. "Thanks for saying that."

"Save your thanks for after, baby," Kell whispered as he slowly pushed deeper inside. Noah wrapped his legs around Kell's hips, his expression slightly dazed as Kell entered him for the first time.

Kell cupped his face, frowning at the intense emotion in Noah's gray eyes. *Let me please him,* he thought, pausing.

"You're the man I love, Kell."

Kell swallowed. "Noah...."

Noah shook his head. "Don't be terrified, Caveman. I knew you loved me when you beat the fuck out of Adam. Violence was your Valentine."

"I do?" Kell felt a bit abashed, like a horny kid caught with a skin mag and a woody.

NOAH kissed him, marveling that there was so little discomfort at taking a man the size of Kell. "You offered to bottom."

Kell winced at the last reminder. "Well, maybe for Christmas." Gently, he began to move. Noah clutched him, hands squeezing, telling him he was wanted. Kell's hand stroked down to where they were joined, palming himself, watching Noah's face, angling his cock. Noah's eyes flared. "Yeah?" Kell whispered.

"*Oh!* So that's what you get out of it?"

KELL'S fingers dug into Noah's hips hard, just short of bruising, forgetting Adam, forgetting the gentleness he'd employed because of him. "Fuck, you have the sweetest little ass! I want to bend you over my desk at work, pull down your pants and fuck you. Let's make a date for next Monday morning."

199

"Okay," Noah gasped, hands raking Kell's sweaty back. His expression said it wasn't enough yet. "Kell, let me up."

Kell blinked but then pulled out, and Noah kissed him, showing his appreciation. Well, fuck yeah, because Kell didn't want to leave that tight sweet ass. "Did I hurt you?"

Noah smiled. "No. I want to sit on it. I want to watch it go in. I want to *take* it in, ride it, pretend that it's my job to fuck you, whenever you want, however you want it...."

Kell swore. "*God Almighty,* Noah!"

He sat up on the bed, watching as Noah curled around him, holding Kell's big cock still as he slowly impaled himself on it. "I'm yours," Noah whispered.

"*Noah!*" Kell hammered up, unable to resist. "Fuck, take it. Beautiful. Made to suck cock, made to be fucked by it!"

Noah's tongue came out, teasing as he licked lips swollen from Kell's kisses. He looked fucking amazing full of Kell's prick. "Put your hands on the headboard. Hold onto it while I fuck myself on you," Noah whispered. Kell growled again, muscled arms stretching above his head, his big chest sweaty and heaving as Noah rode him. Noah moved lazily, provocative, Kell shoving up, hands gripping the headboard so they were white.

"*Mine!*" Kell rasped as he shot himself into Noah. God, he never got enough of that.

"Mine," Noah agreed, jerking in spasms as he climaxed happy mess all over his lover's muscled belly.

ALEC was replacing his amulet after removing it for a shower. He hissed and drew his fingers back. His dark eyes widened. "Oh shit!"

"What?" Jade asked, drying his back, putting a timid kiss there. Glowing quietly.

"Dunno. Something bad. I need to talk to Kell, I think."

They both jumped when the phone rang. "Shit!" Jade laughed, reaching for it, dropping the towel. She listened a moment and then handed it to Alec with a frown between her brows. "It's your Grandmother Ruth. She says it's our time to do something, fix the imbalance...."

Chapter 24

NOAH twisted in Kell's arms, restless. He felt a familiar worry, a familiar spike of need to protect Josh. He balled his fists, lost in a dream.

He was in his house, the house he'd bought with Josh for a new start, only it was years ago, the wallpaper fresh, the purple pool unmarred by cracks or corrosion. He walked through the hallways, peering into Josh's room. He saw posters of fighter jets, big trucks... and a boy with black hair and bright blue eyes reading a book on his small bunk bed. He looked up with a smile, which quickly faded to anxiety. "You won't leave me alone again, will you?" he whispered.

Noah felt loss kick him like a punch to the gut. "I'm looking for my son," he said. "You shouldn't be here."

"I know, I don't belong," the boy said sadly.

"Where is Josh?" Noah felt for the boy, but he had to find his son. "Josh!"

"He followed me, of course," the boy replied, getting to his feet, lake-blue eyes holding Noah's seriously. "You better hurry."

Noah jerked awake, coated with sweat. He glanced at the clock. Barely half an hour had passed since he and Kell.... He looked at his sleeping lover, but he couldn't.... What gripped him was sure, singing knowledge, but even now the dream was fading. He could lose his son if he took even a moment to try to explain this strange connection to Kell—even as part of him chided it was only a dream, irrational. But if Josh wasn't in the house as he sensed, he had to find him.

He gently pulled Kell's possessive arm from his waist and climbed off the bed they'd shared, reaching for his pants.

Josh, I'm coming.

ADAM frowned as he exited the SUV that Anderson had provided for him. He hadn't stationed himself on a feeder street near Noah's house for very long when he'd spotted Noah himself tearing out in his Tundra truck. What the fuck…?

Of course, Adam had followed. Doing Anderson's surveillance was all well and fine, but it was *Noah* who had brought him down here to this hick town in the first place.

At first Noah had driven around aimlessly, as if he didn't know where he was going, but then he'd headed down a dirt track. Adam had driven with his heart pounding and his headlights off so the man he was following wouldn't see him.

He'd left his truck and shadowed the path that Adam knew from his reconnaissance led to the abandoned greenhouse owned by the dead pot dealer.

With no idea what was up, Adam didn't want this to get violent. That would be a mistake, but nevertheless, he pulled out his gun and screwed on a silencer.

He wasn't finished with Noah Matthews.

ONCE he arrived in the clearing, Noah wasn't sure what to do. He had no protective, guiding Kell; he'd abandoned his capable lover and followed the thin trail of instinct. What the hell was he doing out here? He recognized the place from the townsfolk's description, but he'd never imagined coming to this place.

Sweat turned icy against his skin as he felt the oppressive woods all around him, as if waiting to swallow him, to watch him die like Morley Orris.

Not knowing what to do, he fell on habit. Lights might make him feel more secure. It took Noah an inordinate amount of screwing around to get Morley Orris's old generator working again. Perspiring and, yeah, a little nervous on the dark side of the mountain, he was relieved once it started chugging, breaking the still, waiting silence of the tall trees. He wasted no time in heading into the greenhouse and snapping on the switch.

"Shit!" he cursed, meeting familiar eyes.

KELL woke from a satisfied doze when his cell rang. There was no sign of Noah, and he frowned, wondering when he'd left the bed. The new possessive side of him didn't like it, not at all. "Farraday." He sat up, hand touching the cool space where Noah had lain. "Shit! Just stay there, I'll come to you!" he barked. "I'll come and get you, so don't leave!"

Kell snatched for his pants, almost ignoring his phone when it rang a second time.

It was Alec. "Yeah?" He listened a second and then outlined. "All right, but I'm heading for the greenhouse. It's Noah, Alec. Noah and Josh."

Kell grabbed his abandoned T-shirt, cold to his bones, goose bumps actually forming on his skin. He had to get it together. For Noah, for Josh. His instincts were screaming this was the end game, everything coming together somehow.

He was distantly aware that his body was still slightly sticky with sweat and come from that first time with Noah as he yanked on clothing. Shit! So much for afterglow.

But by God, he'd be here again, him and Noah with Josh, safe under this roof. Grabbing his keys and gun, Kell barreled out of the room.

NOAH closed his phone, his heavy-duty flashlight gripped in free hand, which was shaking. "Okay, I got our Chief," he told his son, trying to ignore the prickle of warning on the back of his neck, as if finding Josh here was a harbinger of bad things to come. "Josh, are you okay?" He squeezed his kid's shoulder, wanting him to know he wasn't alone.

Josh nodded.

"Why did you leave the house, come here?" Noah wanted to yell at Josh for doing it when he'd ordered him never to come out here on his own, but the same instinct that had guided him to Josh was whispering that maybe Josh had had no choice.

"I got in through the broken window in the back," Josh explained. "Dad, I know you don't want to hear this, but I had to come. I felt like I had a connection to him. Because… I feel a little lost too, coming down here, you with a new boyfriend."

Noah moved the flashlight off Josh's face when his son flinched from the light. He had an idea what he meant, though he still wasn't sure what had lured Josh from his safe bed at the house. But he was going to find out!

A prickle spiked against the back of his neck, and he swung around, his eyes widening at what he saw.

He knelt just outside the open door of the green house, his blue eyes familiar from Noah's dream, long black hair pulled away from his face with a strip of leather. He was bare-chested, weathered brown, wearing patched jeans and homemade moccasins. Across his muscular chest was a scabbard for a large knife.

"AND you were worried about *me* taking it on, whatever has been haunting this mountain, weren't you?" Kell muttered angrily to himself as he got out of his truck, seeing Noah's Tundra parked just ahead. And yet, as he yanked out his shotgun, making sure it was ready to rock, Kell experienced again that leaden feeling of inevitability, as if everything had led to this moment.

But by damn, he wasn't going to find any more bodies. This ended now. He would make his family safe and get to the bottom of this mystery! And then he'd give Noah hell for scaring the shit out of him.

Love him? Jesus H. Christ! Wait till Noah got a load of the love Kell was feeling right now!

"WHO is that?" Noah stared back at the boy, who returned his gaze, cocking his head and tracking Noah's every movement. Noah felt like he was in the presence of a wild animal and not a young man. His throat was dry, his heart thumping hard. The knife scared him. This boy might have killed Morley Orris.

And yet, as he held that lake-blue gaze… there was also a faint wisp of wonder.

"Josh," he breathed, breaking contact long enough to look at his son, who stood frozen, staring at the wild young man in the doorway. "Walk to me."

"Dad, I'm sorry I screwed up," Josh admitted. "I just wanted to help him."

Noah found it hard to look away from those feral blue eyes. Could this young man even talk? How had he come to be out here? "I know you want to help, Josh."

Josh obeyed Noah's earlier command, reaching out to touch his Dad's rigid shoulder, ducking closer as if for safety. Crap. Noah sincerely hoped he'd be able to offer that. He couldn't help remembering that Morley Orris had died in this very clearing.

Noah's hand clenched on his son's shoulder. "I'm going to walk you to the very back of the greenhouse, behind all the tables, *slowly*. When you get free of the greenhouse, hide and wait for Kell," Noah whispered.

"I don't want to leave you," Josh said flatly, stubborn expression moving over his face. "And Wylde needs help too, Dad. It's why he came to us."

"Wylde?" Noah blinked. "Is that his name?"

"I heard a couple of people in town call him that," Josh said. "It seems to suit him and he's not exactly talking."

"No, he's not. Josh, please do as I ask!" Noah felt sweat run down the middle of his back, coat his upper lip and forehead. He had to make sure his kid was safe. It was coming full circle, because Josh's safety was why they'd moved to this town in the first place.

"I followed him through the woods but lost him when I found the green house. But I think he wants to talk to me, to us. I think he's afraid."

Noah listened but still pulled Josh closer, placing an arm around the boy protectively as he inched toward the back end of the greenhouse. "Josh, Kell will be here soon. He'll make us safe," Noah said, hoping very fucking much that would happen. But he could almost feel Kell, sense him coming, feel his determination... and how pissed off his lover would be at Noah taking off.

Josh only shook his head. "Right now it's up to you and me."

From the door, Noah saw the shadowy figure of the young man blur, and then he was airborne, leaping onto the closest metal table, crouching, closer to him and Josh, confronting them. His hand gripped the knife scabbard.

"For God's sake, *don't move!*" Noah rasped, freezing, feeling like prey fixed in the gaze of a predator.

"I've been doing some reading," Josh continued gravely, as if he and Noah were back home at their house with their elaborate security system and not in a space belonging to a dead man, trapped by a young wild man.

Noah maneuvered Josh carefully into place behind him. They'd reached the back of the greenhouse, and the broken window was there, cool night air making Noah's shirt chill where it stuck to his skin.

Behind him, ceramic pots clattered. The boy was tearing apart the remainder of the dying little crop from the dead pot dealer, making sounds of frustration. Fine with Noah, since it meant he and Josh could make their escape.

"I think he wants to talk to us but he's forgotten how. He's very sad," Josh said.

"You may be right, but your new friend is a little unpredictable."

"If I'm right does that mean I get those driving lessons early?" Josh joked weakly.

The window. Noah had to get his kid through the window. He nudged Josh closer.

"Sssssstttt," the wild boy was whispering. He was huddled on the table, rocking now. "Sssteeee."

"He's trying to talk to us," Josh said. "Dad, we need to help him!"

Don't think. Get Josh through the damn window. Noah hefted his son up, moving him onto the sill. "I'll be fine. Once you are outside, try to hide somewhere and don't move. Kell will be here any minute."

"And leave you with Wylde?"

"I'll do my best to avoid that knife, don't worry," Noah promised. He figured if he stayed away from the young man, he wouldn't feel threatened.

"I want someone to help him. Will Kell help him? I think Wylde's been alone a long time," Josh said, edging outside. When his son fell to the other side, to safety, Wylde let out a high, undulating sound, and Noah stilled, watching him.

The young man leaped even closer, startling Noah, scattering dying marijuana plants, wide blue eyes fixed on him as Noah mashed himself against the trembling broken glass wall in a probably futile-as-hell gesture. If Wylde wanted to hurt him, he could.

"Steeev-an," Wylde whispered, lifting up one scarred palm. "Steven."

Noah froze, listening now. Like Josh said, the young man did not seem to want to hurt him. He wanted to communicate.

"Steven? That's your name?" Noah repeated. "Oh, God, son, how long have you been out here?"

Steven's lips moved, as if he was trying to understand Noah's words by mouthing them. His eyes filled with tears. "Long…."

Suddenly the broken green house door swung open on its hinges. Kell!

Not Kell, but Adam! Muscled, confident, gun raised. He paused, and his eyes widened as he took in the young man, whose head whipped around in his direction. Wylde put his hand instinctively on his knife scabbard.

"*Holy fuck!*" Adam pointed his gun. Fired.

Noah heard a coughing sound. Blood sprayed glass, and Wylde gave a hoarse cry, grabbing his shoulder.

"*Don't hurt him!*" Noah yelled.

Chapter 25

A BALLET of death, Noah thought. Freakish choreography, blood running down broken shards of glass, the tight face of the wild man, silent agony burning in the blue eyes.

Noah had never seen anyone move so fast: One moment Wylde was crouched, hurting. The next he leaped through the air, knife raised—

Suddenly Josh was there, behind Adam, Noah's worst nightmare. *Oh, God!* Josh shoved Adam—

"*No!*" Noah screamed, thrusting the knocked-over steel table aside in an insane bit of choreography of his own. Josh. Josh and Adam. Josh and Wylde.

Wylde struck him in passing, intent on Adam.

Josh yelled, wide, terrified gray eyes so like his own holding Noah's in horror. "No, not Dad. *Don't hurt!*"

For a second, Wylde's gaze riveted on Josh while Adam was frantically feeding a clip into his gun with shaking fingers. Then the young man made a soft sound and leaped through the broken window, disappearing into the night.

At the same time, Noah flung himself on Adam, struggling for his weapon, determined the other man wouldn't shoot any more bullets with his child in the greenhouse.

"You ungrateful little fuck. I'm saving you," Adam snarled.

Noah struck Adam with his elbow. "Saving me, my ass!"

"That's my job!"

Kell!

Kell's boot crushed Adam's gun hand to the littered floor. The man glared up at the Chief with hate and bruises shining on his pale, sweating face.

"What took you so long?" Noah rasped, taking in his big man, the shotgun he carried, every inch the protective warrior as he stood in the destroyed greenhouse. Oh, yes, definitely his Alpha male.

Suddenly Noah felt safe, even if he wondered how he and Josh would make a life here after everything that had happened since they'd come to Sullivan's Mountain. But that was something for him and Kell to resolve. Maybe he'd take up his boyfriend's offer and move in with Kell. He'd never entertained the idea before, dismissing it automatically since he liked his independence, but now it seemed so simple. Who cared where they lived as long as they were together and safe?

Kell kicked away Adam's weapon and then gestured with his firearm. "Up against the wall." His narrowed eyes said, *Give me a reason, asshole.*

"Now just a fucking minute!" Adam huffed. "Do you even have jurisdiction here, Chief? And I have done nothing wrong, other than hunting that wild boy—everyone in town will be happy he's not a danger anymore."

"Do it." Kell kept his eyes on Adam, his gun ready, but something in his pose demanded Noah come to him.

Noah reached for Adam's weapon first and emptied it. He saw a sizzle of primitive satisfaction at his small act of prowess in Kell's eyes. It did seem to turn on his big macho man when Noah showed his strength. Kell wasn't afraid of it; he enjoyed it, encouraged it.

Noah was fortunate he'd met the impossible man.

"You all right?" Kell demanded. He swallowed visibly, and Noah could see how scared he'd been. Likely they would soon have a mother of an argument, but hopefully the occasion would never

211

come up again for Noah to take off without letting his… partner know. But now he had to make one thing clear.

"Fine now you're here. And Kell, it wasn't because you aren't family that I left without talking to you first. It was…." He shook his head, not sure how to put into words the dream, the strange certainty he'd followed that had led him to Josh. "Peculiar, what happened tonight."

Kell glanced around the room. Noah had the impression a large helping of his awareness was still on Adam, ready to take him on if he so much as twitched. Well, on that score they were in agreement; Adam had put Josh at risk. "I'd say 'peculiar' is one word for it." Kell's face tightened. "Shit! Where's Josh?"

JOSH hesitated on the rim of the canyon wall. The sun was rising, dawn coming at last. In the dim growing light, he made out what looked like a dark blotch on the rounded granite. When he crouched to touch it, it wet his fingers. *Blood.*

Wylde had certainly come this way. And something told him if he followed, he'd finally be able to help the young man, bring him home. He just hoped his Dad wouldn't totally freak. Man, he'd never be allowed to borrow the Tundra at this rate, which totally sucked!

He knew from eavesdropping a couple of times when deputy Alec Danvers had talked to Kell that there was some kind of shelter in the canyon below. Maybe where Wylde had lived for a long time, on his own?

He took a deep breath. *Do this, and it could be over*, his instincts whispered. Pebbles skittered under his running shoes as he climbed down into darkness.

"WHAT are you going to do?" Adam jeered. "Go after that kid? You're going to fucking die, Chief. He's the same killer you've been looking for and he's going to fucking rip you open and I can't wait!"

Kell's jaw was rock hard as he clicked the handcuffs closed, fixing Adam to a steel pipe attached to the generator.

Then he got in Adam's face, wishing that he could get into it with him fully again, but right now he had better things to do. It couldn't be too soon until local deputies arrived and could take custody of the asshole. "Maybe not. Maybe while I'm in the woods, he'll come back and visit you first."

Adam's eyes widened in horror. "Fuck you! Get back here, you fucking bastard!"

Kell shook his head at Noah, who was checking his own shotgun, his face still, fixed and pale. "You should wait here for Alec."

"No," Noah said flatly. "Don't tell me I'll slow you down. Don't tell me it's dangerous. Or, as Adam said, fuck you!"

KELL strode close enough to grip Noah's neck, pulling him near a bit like he was a puppy, but the hard kiss he gave him was one of equals. Noah's hand clenched on his arm. He knew that the other man regretted he wasn't easy so he could demand Noah stay safe.

But Noah was reassured on a primitive level. His caveman had just made a silent promise.

We'll find him. We'll make him safe.

"Let's get going," Kell said.

"THAT boy was so scared," Noah mused softly as he ran alongside of Kell. His new lover was an amazing tracker, finding Josh's footprints, charging after him like a cougar on the hunt. With every stride, Noah felt they were getting closer, that they would find Josh. "Could he really have hurt someone?"

"I don't know. I hope not."

Noah shook his head. "This whole town let that boy down for years. Somehow he fell through the cracks and no one took him home."

"He'll come home now, Noah, one way or another," Kell promised. "Meantime, looks like he's gone to ground since he's wounded. This trail leads to the canyon."

JOSH'S eyes widened as he stepped carefully over brush and a large log that looked freshly rolled. He pushed aside some blackberry bushes, dead branches and curled leaves warmed through by the light from the rising sun, which was now throwing golden coloring onto the red-and-gray-stained canyon wall.

Scraps of cloth. A little firepit. Dew seeped down, dripping a pattern of spattering tears on the loose rock. Moving closer, Josh placed his hand on warming rock, seeing another fading bloody print. Wylde had been here. Put his hand where Josh now had his palm.

And then he saw it. A little shelter of stretched clear plastic, scavenged from somewhere. Wylde was huddled with his head over his knees, pain living in his blue eyes. When he saw Josh, he whispered, "Ste-Steven."

Josh swallowed thickly. And here he'd worried that his Dad wouldn't be there for him. Noah would never let this happen to Josh. "I don't think you ever hurt anyone. You're just... lost," he said. "But you know you can't stay here, Steven."

Josh held out his hand.

ALEC pulled up in his SUV, scattering pebbles. He got out and went
to the back, opening it to retrieve what he'd brought. "If we have to
search that whole canyon for the boys… I brought supplies," he told
Kell, who was watching, sweaty, huffing, obviously having run up
here over hard ground.

"Wait up here for the rest of the volunteers from town. I have
to head down into the canyon with Noah," Kell said.

"I'll stay here and help Alec," Jade offered. "Hey, you better
hurry up and catch Noah!"

"Well, hell!" Kell growled, lunging down the path Noah was
already following that led down the crack into the canyon.

RETRACING his steps, Josh reached up to balance himself. He'd
found Wylde—Steven—and somehow he had to talk to the Chief,
get him to understand.

"And just where do you think you're going, young man?" a
crisp voice called.

Josh froze, taking an instinctive step back away from the tall
man with bleak gray eyes who was cradling a rifle.

"You saw him, didn't you? Is he hiding close by? He's a killer
and he has to be stopped."

"Leave him alone!" Josh growled. "Haven't you done
enough?"

The man blinked. "Has that creature talked? You can't believe
what he says."

"Steven didn't hurt Morley Orris, but *you* did. He saw it
happen! And he's been scared ever since."

"A man has a right to protect his family. Orris was
blackmailing my wife over her affair with the unfortunate Ralph

Hindle." Anderson smiled bleakly. "My family isn't so different from yours. We came here for a fresh start… only Marisa can't seem to help herself."

"Did you… kill Ralph Hindle too? Kill him and make it look like wild animals and then make the rest of his family leave our house?" Josh prodded. "Everyone in town thought they'd run away from the ghost."

"Your 'Steven' has been most helpful in that regard," Anderson said. "People are predictably frightened of anyone different and he's an outsider. Tell me, where is he?"

Josh dropped to the ground instinctively, falling away, heart pounding. Steven had been right behind him, but he was bleeding, hurting—Josh had to lead Anderson away from him. He knew Kell and his Dad would come for him.

Chips of rocks exploded as Anderson fired. "Just tell me where he is and I'll let you go."

"Yeah, right," Josh growled under his breath.

Chapter 26

NOAH relaxed minutely when Kell reached his side, rejoining him in their search.

"We're almost at that shelter that Jade and Alec found," Kell said.

Noah had one focus: find Josh. Kell squeezed his hand for a moment as if understanding.

"I can hear dripping," Kell continued in a hushed voice. "Just ahead. Watch your footing on that loose shale."

"*Josh!*" Noah called softly.

Suddenly, gunfire erupted. It struck the rock wall, sending chips through the air like shrapnel.

"*Down!*" Kell's big body hammered him against the canyon. The flashlight they'd carried to illuminate the dark corners bounced away, sending crazy splashes of light onto the walls.

"*Kell!*" Noah saw Kell was clutching his thigh, hand wet and glistening. *Blood.*

Kell's face was tight. "Noah, I can't move fast with this, so it's down to you." He took a breath. "S-someone's coming, so look sharp!"

Noah also caught the sounds of hurried footfalls. "Josh's out there… and the shooter!"

Kell nodded, grimacing as he tore the bottom of his shirt. When awkwardly he tried to tie it around his leg, Noah took it with an annoyed sound, tying it for him.

"ANCIENT Roman coins and mammoths were found in the New World," Alec noted, pacing above the canyon wall, waiting. It was hard to do that, but someone had to be here in case Josh showed up. "There are still a lot of mysteries, so a boy like Wylde running away to live in the woods after his grandfather passed away isn't that strange. The old man died of a heart attack. To a little kid, that must have been very frightening."

"So somehow we missed him, lost track of him," Jade agreed, wiping off her hands on her jeans. "Except I knew I was feeding someone with the cookies I put out. I mentioned it to the librarian once at the diner and she said a lot of women in town did the same, left food or clothing out for him. Alec, are you thinking what I am, that we need to step up and take care of him?"

"Yep." Alec chewed his lip, obviously worrying about what was happening in the canyon below. "He must be just over twenty years of age now, Jade, but he's innocent, lost. He'll need someone to protect him."

"You know, for so long, all I wanted was to get out of this hick town," Jade mused. She looked at Alec under her brows. "But maybe… since you and that kid need me, I'll stick."

"Okay then," Alec said, smile touching his lips.

They both stiffened as they caught the sound of gunfire from the canyon below.

"I SEE you decided to cooperate, very good," Anderson said, smiling as he cornered Josh against the canyon wall. "Once the boy is dead, everything will go back to normal. The townsfolk could have rescued him years ago, but they looked away. They'll do it again."

"*Josh!*"

Josh sagged as he spotted his father coming around a rounded pillar of granite. He felt his own face soften, his stomach roiling vulnerability, dread, relief. "Oh, shit, Dad!"

"I just want the wild kid," Anderson began, waving his gun. "And then I'll let your boy free."

Noah fired. Anderson cried out, dropping his weapon and grabbing his arm. Red, misty blood shadowed the canyon wall behind him. "But you didn't warn me you were going to shoot!" Anderson grumbled, outraged as he slid down to his ass.

"Why would I do that?" Noah's face was rock hard. He watched as Josh picked up Anderson's gun, and then he raised his free arm; despite being twelve and a little too independent lately for Noah's peace of mind, Josh nestled close, giving his father the hug he really needed.

A moment later, a figure moved from the forest. Noah held his breath, looking into shadowed blue eyes. But then Wylde made up his mind at last, and, clutching his shoulder, walked to where Noah and Josh were waiting for him.

KELL glanced over his shoulder at the ambulance taking Anderson under guard to the nearest E.R. For a moment he relived the white flash of joy he'd experienced when he'd seen the man appear along with Josh and Noah… and Wylde, though he would have to get used to calling him Steven, he guessed. Steven Butler, lost grandson of the first owner of Noah's house.

Noah had helped Kell navigate his way back up the crack, patient with Kell's swearing. His leg hurt, damn it! But he was good to go for one final mission to put an end to this.

He hefted the knife he'd taken from Wylde. It wasn't African in origin like the killer's blade. He wagered they'd find that in Anderson's possession. The man had killed Morley for blackmail and most likely left the word "don't" in his own garage—a warning to his cheating wife. He'd also tried to use the townspeople's fear to point a finger at innocent Wylde.

"Guess we don't have to worry about insanely territorial husbands thanks to your boyfriend Wyatt Earp," Alec teased laconically, shooting an amused glance at Noah, who had an arm around Josh as they stood at the canyon's edge.

"Are you sure you're ready for this, Alec?" Kell prodded, not wanting to say he would have aimed for Anderson's balls if it had been up to him. He wanted this over with because he was hurting, and he wanted to be patched up and back in Noah's house eating tofu by this evening. At least the dessert tofu wasn't so bad. He'd discovered he liked the strawberry flavor.

The ambulance driver had wanted to take him in along with Anderson, but he'd put it off for the moment, wanting to be sure his friend knew what he was getting into. "The social worker should meet you at Jade's house, and there will be a lot of paperwork, a lot to go through if you want to help Wylde—I mean, Steven."

"Jade and I would like to try," Alec said peaceably. "My Grandmother Ruth said it was to be our role, restoring balance. By the way, I just heard from the county deputies in the clearing. Adam is also in custody."

Kell nodded with satisfaction. He had a feeling that Noah's ex would be in hot water once Anderson shared what they'd been up to. And that man struck him as someone who would definitely want to make a deal; he was a superlative businessman, after all, even if he was nuts.

"One thing, I think Wylde is gay," Kell said. "Just a vibe I caught, not that the poor kid probably gets it. Is that a problem?" He had to ask.

Alec said, "Nope."

"Okay, then." Kell limped over to Josh and Noah, putting an arm around them both. As a foster kid, he had never had a family, never thought he'd miss it, but now he'd come home, and it looked like Steven had come home at last too.

"How are you holding up?" Noah asked gently, gray eyes moving over Kell's tight face.

Kell pressed a kiss against Noah's mouth, silently telling him not to worry. "Just want to head home now, you know."

Noah sighed. "Oh yes."

"Start that new life with my new man," Kell continued, teasing.

"I was thinking maybe we might move down into your house."

Kell shrugged. "I don't care where we live, but I only have one bathroom and no pool, not even a crumbling purple one."

"Um. And probably no copper-plated appliances," Noah added wistfully. "No peppermill to grind fresh peppercorns...."

"Nope. I'm not sure I have anything more than the basics."

"But I *like* your basics." Noah's eyes twinkled.

"Sheesh," Josh muttered, rolling his eyes at the romantic exchange. "Obviously you read those Victorian books I lent you on courting." He gave Kell an amused look, liking that it was returned by a glint in the Chief's eye. He kept his possessive arm around Josh's Dad.

"Wylde—Steven, is going to be okay, Josh. You can stand down on his account, though I'm sure he'll need a friend."

"The right people are going to help him, Chief?" Josh asked, a little anxious on that score.

"Absolutely. Your Dad and I will make sure." Kell's arm was still around Noah, as if saying he wasn't going anywhere. "Initially he'll be staying with Jade and Alec since it's close to the forest where he grew up. It wasn't easy to arrange for that but I have some pull and a lot of folks in town are supporting it."

And Josh relaxed, knowing it would be okay now. "You know, Steven told me the purple pool was his idea," he shared. "It's his favorite color."

KELL nodded to Alec as Alec headed back to his SUV with Jade and Steven. They were going to take Steven to the local E.R. for his shoulder and then take him home to Jade's house. Those two were really going to be an item now, and Kell was sure he'd hear all about them and their new houseguest from various townspeople over his peach pie at the diner. He looked forward to it.

"I still have to give Fiona a bath," Josh said, looking sleepy. "But maybe I can have a nap first."

"Good idea," Noah said. "Maybe we'll all do that once Kell is patched up." Noah raised his brows at Kell, giving him a pointed look. Yeah, looked like he'd be in the E.R. soon too.

"I have another bike-a-thon I need to do traffic control on," Kell said, rubbing his eyes. Life was settling back down, and he was more than ready for traffic control as opposed to eerie searches in the woods.

Josh got in the back of Kell's SUV while Noah helped Kell carefully into the passenger side, taking care not to bump his bandaged leg. Liking being spoiled, Kell nuzzled the sleek ash-blond hair and whispered the words he knew Noah most wanted to hear.

JAN IRVING has worked in all kinds of creative fields, from painting silk to making porcelain ceramics, to interior design, but writing was always her passion.

She feels you can't fully understand characters until you follow their journey through a story world. Many kinds of worlds interest her, fantasy, historical, science fiction and suspense—but all have one thing in common, people finding a way to live together—in the most emotional and erotic fashion possible, of course!

Visit Jan's blog at http://jan-revealed.livejournal.com.

Don't miss these stories by JAN IRVING

http://www.dreamspinnerpress.com